Chasing Abby

Shattered Hearts Series Book Four

CASSIA LEO

CHASING ABBY

Copyright © 2014 by Cassia Leo

First Edition. All rights reserved.

Cover art by Sarah Hansen at Okay Creations.
Copyedited by Marianne Tatom.

ISBN-13: 978-1500279301
ISBN-10: 1500279307

Chasing Abby

For all the Shattered Hearts.

Note to Reader

Music is an important part of this series. Some chapters in this book begin with a musical note. The musical note indicates there is a song on the *Chasing Abby* playlist that pertains to or is mentioned in that chapter. Please feel free to open the playlist on a computer or mobile device and listen as you read.

The playlist is available on YouTube at:
bit.ly/chasingabbyplaylist

The playlist is available on Spotify at:
bit.ly/chasingabbyplaylists

PROLOGUE

Four months after

MY HAND IS SHAKING as I jam the key into the ignition. The smell of leather is making me even more nervous. I've never driven a car this expensive. Actually, I've hardly driven any car of any value. I'm not sure I can safely drive Jimi's Mercedes. If I crash today, I guess I can thank my fabulous parents and their need to protect my fragile heart.

I turn the key and the engine hums. I shift into reverse and punch the gas pedal, then I nearly pass out when the car jumps backward into the driveway, almost crashing into the block wall separating the beach house from the neighbor's house. My mom comes bounding out of the front door. I quickly switch gears and peel out of the driveway onto Sandpiper Street, then I head toward Lumina Avenue.

I don't know if anyone will follow me. I hope they don't. I just need to get away.

For eighteen years, I was the sickly, fragile daughter of Brian and Lynette Jensen. Now... I don't know who I am. When I'm with my biological parents, I don't feel like the frail girl I was eight weeks ago. I'm different. I'm the girl who got away. The girl who was strong enough to capture my parents' hearts in a single twenty-minute meeting and hold them captive for eighteen years.

That's the girl I want to be. I don't want to be fragile anymore.

I turn left on Lumina and the Mercedes grips the slick asphalt beautifully. Racing forward, I turn right onto Highway 74 and draw in a deep breath. I don't know where I'm going. All I know is that I can't be there right now. I need to think without my mom's pitiful gaze penetrating me. Or the look of disappointment and hope in Chris and Claire's eyes.

I touch the power button on the touchscreen and Jimi's favorite playlist begins to play. I listen to the beachy, acoustic melodies and think the past few weeks. Flashes of my parents' hopeful faces flicker in my mind. Caleb's face materializes, and memories of that day on the beach come rushing back to me. My body relaxes and my hands stop trembling as a smile curls my lips. Caleb is my constant.

Even when I'm being pulled this way and that way, it's Caleb's face, his sturdy hands, his breath so soft on my skin, his love so fragile in my hands… Caleb is the rope that keeps me tethered to reality. As long as I have Caleb, I'll get through this.

A buzzing noise pulls me out of my thoughts and I glance at the cup holder between the seats. My phone is flashing. I pick it up and glance at the screen. It's Caleb.

I heave a deep sigh and answer. "Hello?"

When I turn my attention back to the road, something is wrong. The lane has moved. Or… Oh, no. It's not the lane. It's my car that's veered into oncoming traffic. The last thing I hear is Caleb screaming my name before I drop the phone.

PART ONE:

The Jensens

"The hardest part is
knowing when to let go."

CHAPTER ONE

Two months after

THE HAIRS ON MY ARMS stand on end the moment I step inside Fidelity Bank in Raleigh. As if I can feel every time my parents walked through here over the past eighteen years. See the ghost of their footprints trailed across the speckled tile.

Caleb squeezes my hand as we head for the line of patrons queued up in front of the teller windows. I want to smile at him to show him that everything is okay, but I'm too nervous. My heart is pounding like a snare drum inside my chest. My fingers begin to tingle and I know I should stop and take a few deep breaths, but I can't stop moving toward that line. I wriggle my fingers a little and Caleb tightens his grip, stopping in the middle of the floor as he recognizes the signs.

I look up into his green eyes and his eyebrows shoot up as he draws in a deep breath. I copy him, sucking in a large breath through my nostrils then letting it out slowly through my mouth. He does it a few more times and I follow along until the tingling in my fingers is gone. Then I blink my eyes to stanch the tears. It's not fair to Caleb that he has a broken girlfriend. He deserves a girl with a healthy heart who can keep up with his lust for life.

"Better?" he asks, his voice soothing and hopeful.

I nod and he kisses my forehead. "Thank you."

What is it like having a defective heart? Sort of like having a defective TV that only displays a few channels. You're forced to listen to your friends talking about all the cool shows they've been watching. Shows you'll never be able to watch. And you try to pretend you're perfectly happy with your defective TV, but everyone knows you're just trying to be a good sport.

Sports. That's one thing you can't watch on a defective TV. I learned that when I was thirteen. That also happens to be the age I learned about the safe-deposit box that brought me to Fidelity Bank today.

"I can help the next person in line."

I look up and the woman behind the bulletproof

glass is giving me that impatient, eyebrows-raised look. I step forward with Caleb and slip my driver's license into the curved slot on the counter.

"I'm here to... to look at my safe-deposit box." Look at? She must think I'm crazy.

She takes my driver's license and swipes it through a machine. She types in a few commands, then she looks back and forth between the picture on my ID and my face.

"Do you have your key?"

"Yes," I reply quickly as I begin digging in the front pocket of my jeans for the small silver key my father gave me two months ago.

I slide it into the slot and she smiles. "You can hold onto it." She slides my ID back to me and I take both the card and the key back. "Just give me a moment. I have to go get my supervisor to help you."

She disappears behind a curved wall and comes back with a man in a suit who's sifting through a gaggle of keys on a chain as he walks. They arrive at the teller window and the man smiles at me.

He nods to his right. "This way, ma'am."

Ma'am? I've never been called *that* before. I guess this is what it feels like to be an adult.

We reach an unmarked door that buzzes softly

before it's pulled inward. The man with the keys smiles as he waves us inside. He closes the door behind us, then he leads us to an enormous circular vault door. He slips a key into a lock, then he places his thumb on a print reader. A soft beep sounds and he enters a code on a touchpad. A heavy click sounds inside the door and he turns the wheel to open the door and pull it out.

The vault door opens onto a corridor, which runs perpendicular. Straight ahead of us is a room where another heavy, rectangular vault door stands open, revealing a narrow room lined from floor to ceiling with brass safe-deposit boxes. I look right and see more vault doors leading to other places. The man with the keys leads us forward to the room with the safe-deposit boxes. There aren't any tables, just a single plastic chair with metal legs pushed up against the back wall of the narrow room. I may need that.

"Do you know which box is yours?" the man asks.

I look up into his dark eyes and my mind blanks, so Caleb speaks for me. "Fifteen-five-zero-eight."

I nod in agreement and the man smiles as I hold up my key, still unable to speak.

He leads us to the middle of the room and taps a box on the left. "This is it." He begins walking back toward the door. "Go ahead and take your time. When you're ready, just press this button right here and someone will come back to let you out."

I nod again. "Thank you."

He nods as he closes the rectangular vault door, closing us into the room. My fingers are beginning to tingle again, but I don't wriggle them. I don't want to worry Caleb.

I hand him the key. "You open it."

"Do you want me to look inside and tell you what I see?"

"Yes, please."

He looks at me for a moment, then he heads for the back of the room. He carries the chair back to me and pats the seat. I sit down and try to resist the urge to wring my hands.

"Deep breaths, Abby," he reminds me.

"Just open it. I need this over with."

He quickly slides the key into the lock and turns. He pulls box 15508 out of the slot and I lean forward to put my head between my knees. I don't want to see until I know what's in there.

"It's a memory card and… Holy shit."

"What?" My head snaps up, but I can't see inside the box from this angle. "What is it?"

His eyes are wide, but I can't tell if he's excited or terrified.

"Caleb! Answer me. What is it?"

"It's… There are some pictures in here."

"Pictures? So… what? Why is that shocking?"

His Adam's apple bobs in his throat as he gulps. "It's not the pictures that are shocking… It's who's *in* the pictures."

"What? Let me see." I stand up to get a look at the contents of the brass box, but Caleb quickly slides it back into the slot. "What are you doing?"

"You asked me to tell you what I saw *before* you see it."

I slap his arm in frustration. "Then tell me, damn it!"

"Abby, calm down."

He looks into my eyes with that stern look that only Caleb and my dad can pull off.

I take a deep breath and nod. "Okay, I'm calm. What's in the box?"

"It looks like… your biological father is… Chris Knight."

I narrow my eyes at him. "What? Is that supposed to be a joke? Because that is not funny at all. Just tell me what's inside the box."

He's not smiling as his eyes lock on mine. "This is not a joke."

The silence is so absolute, I can hear my feeble heart stuttering under the weight of this news.

"Sit down, baby," he whispers and I gladly sit as he pulls the box out of the slot again. "Are you ready?"

I nod and he carefully sets the box in my lap. The first thing I see is the picture sitting on top of the stack. It's clearly a professional family photo. Chris Knight, his wife, and their three kids are standing in front of a large elm tree. They look so happy and... perfect. I'll bet all the TVs in their house work perfectly.

Caleb kneels in front of me and reaches forward to wipe a tear from my cheek. "Are you okay?"

I shake my head, shaking loose another tear. "No."

I lift the photos out of the box and move the top picture to the bottom of the stack. The next one stops me cold. It's a picture of Chris Knight looking quite a bit younger. He's dressed in a suit and holding... me.

CHAPTER TWO

Lynette

Five years before

BRIAN HOLDS OUT A BOTTLE of water to me and I push it away. It's offensive. How can he even think of *my* needs when Abby is out there burning up on the soccer field?

I march toward Coach Fred, but the moment he sees me he shakes his head in dismay and turns his attention back to the field, as if I don't exist. "She needs to come out! Take her out!"

I don't care if all the parents are rolling their eyes. They find me annoying. That much has been obvious from the moment I set foot on the soccer field for Abby's first game six months ago.

Abby had been begging me to let her play a sport, but the only two sports she was interested in were soccer and basketball. Well, I've heard enough horror stories about basketball players with bad hearts collapsing on the court and never waking up. I denied her request for two years until I couldn't take the begging anymore. I told her I'd let her play soccer if she played a defensive position. I didn't factor the Carolina humidity into my decision.

It may be the end of November, but Abby's asthma always acts up more during cool weather. And if she's having trouble breathing, she's going to pass out soon. Her heart just isn't equipped to deal with that kind of stress.

She's standing two hundred feet away from me and, even from this distance, I can see her cheeks are a vibrant red and her mouth is hanging open with exhaustion. But she's one of the team's best defenders, so Coach Fred thinks I'm overreacting. She couldn't play so well if there was anything wrong with her, right?

Wrong. Abby may look like a normal, slightly smaller-than-average thirteen-year-old girl, but she is far from normal, as much as she hates being reminded of that. Right now, her heart is being crushed under the task of trying to keep her body cool and pump oxygen into her lungs. She's going to pass out if I don't get her off that field.

Coach Fred turns to me, his already wrinkled lips pursed in severe disapproval, a look that probably worked on recruits when he was in the military, but it doesn't intimidate me one bit. "There is one minute and forty seconds left in the game."

"I don't care. Call a timeout."

"Mrs. Jensen, I am going to have to ask you to please let me do my job. These kids have been working too long for this."

"Lynette, come on." Brian clasps his large hand around the crook of my elbow. "It's almost over."

"Are you kidding me?" I wrench my arm free and shoot him a scathing glare.

The referee's whistle blows and we all turn toward the field. Abby is holding up her arm, the way they're taught to do if they're injured. I manage to take three steps onto the field before she collapses on the grass.

I race toward her, but Brian and the referee beat me there. Brian immediately pours cool water on her face and chest as I dial 911. We've never had to deal with this particular scenario before, but we've had to call an ambulance enough times to have the routine down. Brian roars at the crowd forming around us to disperse.

"She needs air! Move back!"

I fall to my knees next to her, spouting off the location and the facts to the 911 operator. "Eastgate Park, the east side entrance on Wingate Drive. Thirteen-year-old female with severe heatstroke."

"No, not heatstroke!" Brian bellows. "Cardiac arrest! She's in cardiac arrest!"

CHAPTER THREE

Brian

AS I STAND NEXT TO Abby's hospital bed, all I can think is, if I knew thirteen years ago what I know now, I'd have done everything differently with her birth parents. I was thirty-three years old when Chris and Claire Knight came to us asking to change the closed adoption into an open adoption. I wasn't young, but I was foolish. Foolish to think Abby would never need them. Foolish to think *we* would never need them.

Lynette stands next to me, gently stroking the back of Abby's hand with her thumb, the way she has every day for the past seventeen days since Abby collapsed during that soccer game. It wasn't the first time my little girl had passed out from overexertion. Abigail was born with an AV (atrioventricular) canal defect: a gaping hole in her heart.

After the surgery she underwent at the age of five months, her recovery seemed to be going well. Then, we noticed four-year-old Abby struggling to breathe while chasing Harley, our Jack Russell terrier, around the yard. Sure enough, we took her to the doctor and they discovered one of the valves in her heart had begun to weaken and her body wasn't getting enough oxygen. Abby had one more surgery to reshape the leaflet, during which she was technically dead for three minutes and twenty-four seconds. We vowed to do everything we could to prevent her from ever needing surgery again.

Unfortunately, this means Abby has been forced to take various medications for years. We knew this came with a risk of injury to her liver and kidneys. We didn't know—we *couldn't* know—when she switched medications four weeks ago that she's genetically predisposed to liver toxicity due to the way her body synthesized the new drug. This time, it wasn't the stress on her heart that made her collapse. Cardiac arrest was secondary to the most pressing issue: liver failure.

But as I watch her lying in the hospital bed, lost in

the haze of sedation with a tube buried in her throat, I almost wish it were her heart. At least then I'd know that there's some kind of surgery that could fix her.

There is no surgery that can fix Abby's liver. They attempted to reverse the toxicity with corticosteroids, but she's only gotten worse. If she doesn't get a new liver, she could be dead in days. Her best chance at survival, due to her heart condition, is to find a genetic liver donor.

I squeeze Lynette's shoulder and she sniffs loudly. "We have to contact them. We have to at least try," I whisper.

She shakes her head. "What will she think of us when she knows we lied to her?"

"She won't think anything of us if she dies."

"Stop that," she whispers, her voice strangled by the truth of these words.

"It's true. We need them whether we like it or not, and... she needs more from them than a piece of their liver."

Just saying these words aloud fills me with a level of regret so heavy and palpable I feel as if I might collapse from the realization. I grit my teeth and attempt to swallow the lump that forms in my throat. I'm no longer the one person my little girl needs more than anyone.

Reaching forward, I pull a few strands of hair away from the tape holding Abby's breathing tube in place. I want her to look her best for the photograph I'm about to take, quite possibly the most important photograph of her life. And she'll be sleeping right through it. The moment I touch her warm cheek, her head twitches and Lynette pulls my hand back. She doesn't want me to touch Abby's face. She thinks it introduces germs into her nose and mouth and she's afraid of what will happen if they have to give Abby antibiotics.

"I thought we wouldn't have to tell her until she's eighteen. I just don't think I'm ready," Lynette whispers as she reaches for the camera, which rests on the chair beside her. She holds the camera out for me to take, but she doesn't let go when I attempt to grab it. "Wait. Let me fix her hair."

I can hardly breathe as I watch Lynette smooth down Abby's blonde hair. As similar as Abby's hair color is to Lynette's, she doesn't really resemble either one of us. She has brown eyes while Lynette's and mine are blue. She noticed this a few years ago and when she inquired about it, Lynette's response was "Because you got all our best traits. That's why you're so much prettier than us."

You don't have to share DNA with your child to know when they're suffering. Whether Lynette admits it to herself or me, the truth is that Abby knows she's different. I read about adopted children who grow up feeling unwanted even when their adoptive parents make every effort to show them they are loved. This is one of the main reasons why I was so adamant about not allowing Chris and Claire Knight to have any contact with Abby after her first birthday. I knew that if there were a chance that Abby ever felt unwanted or unloved, she would go running to them. Now, I just want her to feel normal. If meeting them is what will save her life and give her back the sense that she is loved, I'll do anything to give her that.

Lynette wipes tears from her face as she steps away from Abby and I take a step back to get a wider angle of the hospital bed. The lighting in this critical-care room is terrible. This isn't something I ever imagined I would care about in the countless days we've spent in hospital rooms.

I take a few shots, feeling sick with myself as I walk around the bed to see which angle makes her look best. Every year, a few days before Christmas, we drop a memory card containing pictures of Abby into a joint safe-deposit box in Raleigh. The Knights also leave a memory card with pictures of themselves, and I can only assume it's because they haven't given up hope that we'll introduce Abby to them. This is the first year we'll be handing them the pictures in person as we beg them to save our girl.

Finally, I have to stop taking photos when I realize I'm about to lose my composure. Turning away from the hospital bed, I silently ask Abby's forgiveness for photographing her while she's in this state. She hates taking pictures, especially Christmas pictures, unless she's had time to fix her hair and put on a nice outfit. The things thirteen-year-old girls worry about baffle me. I often wonder if she inherited this and all the traits I love so much about her from the Knights.

I turn around and Lynette is holding Abby's hand again. "She's lucky we adopted her," she says. This time her voice is a bit louder than a whisper, as if she's trying to convince me—or herself. "She probably wouldn't have survived this long. She's lucky to have us."

"She needs to see those pictures," I insist, but Lynette doesn't look up or acknowledge my words.

Suddenly, Abby's head jerks a bit harder and her fingers begin to move. My heart races as I rush to her side. Her eyes are still closed as tears begin to slide down her temples.

"What's wrong?" I ask instinctively.

A soft whimper sounds in her throat where the breathing tube prevents her from speaking. She shakes her head, her eyes still closed as the tears come faster.

"Call the doctor!" I shout at Lynette, who is dumbfounded. Abby has been in a coma for seventeen days.

Abby's cries become more high-pitched as she struggles to be heard through the tube. "Don't try to speak, honey. The doctor's coming. Just stay calm. Are you in pain?"

She shakes her head even more adamantly and finally she opens her eyes wide.

"Don't be afraid," I whisper as I reach for her hand, but she slaps my fingers away. "Abby, what's wrong?" She reaches for the tape holding her breathing tube and I grab her hand to stop her. "Don't do that." She leans her head back and her muffled cries cease as she closes her eyes. "Honey, are you okay?"

She squeezes her eyes tightly shut and now it looks as if she's in extreme pain. The nurse rushes in and I lock eyes with her. "I think she's in pain."

Abby's cries begin again and she continues to

shake her head. She wants us to know she is not in pain.

The nurse is confused. "Then what's wrong, dear? Is it the tube in your throat? Because we can't take that out. We'll have to wait for the doctor to get here. He's been paged. Can you wait a few more minutes?"

Lynette wears a guarded smile as she rounds the foot of the bed and reaches for me. She didn't see what I just saw.

Abby's cries grow stronger and the nurse appears worried. "You want a piece of paper to write something down?"

Finally, Abby nods and the nurse quickly leaves the room to retrieve a pen and paper, but Lynette beats her to it. She takes her phone out of her purse, opens up the notes app, and hands it to Abby. As she takes the phone from Lynette, she seems to be refusing to look at her. Her hand shakes as she types a few words then lets the phone drop onto her blanket.

The words on the screen break my heart into a million pieces: *I want to see the pictures.*

CHAPTER FOUR

Lynette

THIS IS THE THIRD family dinner in as many days that Abby has refused to speak to us since we returned from the hospital four days ago. I want to shake her to force her to speak, but I know there's only one thing that will bring back her voice. And I can't give it to her.

She sits across from me, stabbing her dinner salad over and over again, oblivious of the shrill sound her fork makes every time it grates against her plate. She eats quickly, eager to get away from the parents who betrayed her. Brian also remains silent and, for once, I'm not happy about that.

When I met Brian my senior year at UNC Chapel

Hill, he was working as an electrician for a company the university had hired to upgrade the lighting in the campus theater. I was twenty-one, talkative, and thin as paper. He was twenty-five with broad shoulders and hardly spoke a word the first three weeks we dated. There was a quiet gentleness about him that I found so completely enthralling. I wanted to crack open his shell and devour his secrets. He's still a quiet person, but he's been very vocal about Abby's right to know her parents lately.

Still, I wish he would say something instead of just shoveling salad and steak into his mouth. I wish he'd show me just a few words of support. More than anything, though, I wish he'd come off this idea that Abby is old enough to know Chris and Claire Knight. She's only *thirteen*.

She's struggling to push the last few bites of salad into her mouth. She hasn't been able to eat much with the new medication they have her on, but it seems she's determined to put all that food away so she can leave.

Her new meds may make her sick, but they saved her life. Brian didn't want to try this drug, afraid the risk of more liver toxicity outweighed the possibility that she would come back to us. But I was right. And

I'm not the type to say I told you so, but this would be the perfect time to say it. I was right about Abby being too sick to continue playing in that soccer game. I was right to take a risk on this new medication. And I know I'm right about keeping her from meeting her biological parents.

"Stop doing that. You'll make yourself sick," I say, putting down my fork as I've suddenly lost my appetite.

She gags as she swallows the last bite of salad and rises from the table with her plate in hand. She disappears into the kitchen without a word and I stare at her empty chair as I listen to the faucet come on in the kitchen, then the opening and closing of the dishwasher door. Then silence.

I glance at Brian and his elbows are resting on the table as he stares at Abby's empty chair. I want to ask what he's thinking, but I don't want to know. Soon, he stands up and reaches for my plate.

When the dinner dishes are clean, I lean against the counter in the kitchen and Brian leans against the island across from me. I stare at his feet for a moment before I look up. He's wearing that expression I fell in love with twenty years ago, that hardness that masked the vulnerability underneath.

"She'll get over this," I whisper, hardly able to bring myself to say the words aloud. "Eventually, she will get over it."

"Will *we*?"

"Don't say that."

He takes a step forward, his bulky frame towering over me as my back is pressed into the counter. "I don't want to lose either of you," he says gruffly as he lifts my chin. "But it looks like that's exactly what's happening. And you're the only one with the power to stop it. It's not too late to make the right decision, Lynette."

He lets go of my chin and leans over. I close my eyes as I anticipate his lips on mine, but the kiss never comes. When I open my eyes, he's gone.

If I give in to Brian, Abby will find out her birth parents are young, rich, and famous: a rock star and an author. How can a middle-class electrical contractor and stay-at-home mom ever hope to compete with that? I know we're not competing for Abby's love, but that's exactly what it will feel like once Abby finds out their identities. Every time she speaks of them excitedly, I'll wonder if she speaks about us like that to Chris and Claire. And she *will* speak of them that way.

They're practically perfect. They donate millions to

charity; they're in their mid-thirties and still look like they're in their twenties; and they're still madly in love. You can see it in every photo of them ever taken. And the worst part: They live twenty minutes away. She'll be able to see them whenever she wants.

I push off the counter and head upstairs. As I reach the second floor, I hear a sound coming from Abby's bedroom. I tiptoe toward her room then I close my eyes as I listen. She's playing her guitar and my eyes instantly well up with tears when I realize she's singing "Blackbird" by The Beatles, a song about learning to fly with broken wings.

It's the first time I've heard her voice in four days. I want to go in there and hold her and tell her everything will be okay. But if I can't tell her everything, then that will just be a lie. I can't tell her the reason she feels like a caged songbird. I can't let her fly away.

CHAPTER FIVE

I LAY MY GUITAR on top of my bed and grab my laptop off the nightstand. I sit cross-legged as I set the computer on the bed in front of me. Flipping open the screen, I type in my password then open my browser to my bookmarks. I stare at the name of the website for a moment before I click on it: birthrecords.com.

I know my dad's credit-card number. I have it saved in a text file because my dad was tired of giving it to me every time I wanted to download a new movie. But my parents will definitely notice a charge on their account made to birthrecords.com. Then I'll lose my credit-card privileges and they'll probably move us to a remote island in the South Pacific with no Internet access. Well, my dad will probably protest for a couple of days before he gives into my mom, as always.

I open up my "Saved Orders" page and stare at the "Submit" button. Just a few more clicks and I can have the name of the agency that handled my adoption. That doesn't mean they'll give me the names of my birth parents, or that the agency still exists. All it means is that I'll have one more piece of the puzzle. One tiny piece of a puzzle that's missing half its pieces. It may seem insignificant and pointless, but it means the world to me.

Why can't my mother see that?

If I knew what hospital I was born in, or what time I was born, I could go to the county courthouse and search the birth records myself. But my parents have already admitted to lying about this information when I asked them about it years ago in casual conversation.

"Mommy, where was I born?"

"In a hospital, of course."

"What hospital?"

Mom and Dad exchanged shifty looks as they used their ESP to come up with a lie. Always covering their tracks. God forbid I should want to know anything about my true identity.

I wonder if I look more like my biological mom or

dad. I wonder if they play music like me. I wonder if they live here in North Carolina or somewhere cool like New York or Hollywood. I wonder if they broke up or if they had more kids after they gave me up. Maybe I was the only one they didn't want.

Most of all, I just wonder if they ever think of me.

I open up a new tab on my browser and begin a new search: abigail jensen adoption decree. I hit go and, of course, nothing related to me or my parents comes up. But that hasn't stopped me from repeating this same search string a billion times over the past three days. Since *he* gave me the idea.

I open my email next to check for new messages and I'm relieved to find I have two. I already feel like a ghost in this house. I don't think I could handle being invisible to my friends.

I check Amy's message first.

From: amybestest2013@gmail.com
To: abigailjensen13@gmail.com
Subject: Lameness

Vanessa's party isn't gonna be a sleepover anymore. Her parents flipped out when they heard boys were coming. Her parents are the worst.

I chuckle at the last sentence in my best friend's email. She doesn't know what I found out a few days ago. If she knew, she would have to agree that *my* parents are the worst. At least, my mom is.

I type a reply to Amy telling her I'm not sure I'll be able to go to the party anyway. My parents only let me go back to school today because they think it will get me talking to them again. They're afraid of me being around a lot of *germs* while my body is adjusting to the new meds. I hit send then my finger trembles as I click on the next email in the queue.

> From: ceverett0115@gmail.com
> To: abigailjensen13@gmail.com
> Subject: homework
>
> did you take down the page numbers for warner?

I smile at the obvious ploy to start up a conversation. Caleb Everett is the last guy I would expect to email me. He's been sitting next to me in Mr. Warner's algebra class for four months and he hasn't spoken to me all year. Though, I have caught him sneaking glances at me once in a while. I just figured that was the way he was with all girls.

I've never actually had a boyfriend. Not that this is terribly uncommon for girls my age. But I'd be lying if I said I hadn't imagined walking the halls hand-in-hand with Caleb ever since we ran into each other in the hospital four days ago.

I was getting ready to leave my hospital room, but I was still waiting for my parents to bring my street clothes. They were settling the financial stuff down the hall from my room and I was getting pretty impatient. Grabbing the back of my hospital gown to hold it closed, I slid out of bed and tiptoed to the doorway to peer down the corridor. That's when I saw him.

Caleb was running his hand over his messy light-brown hair, his gaze pointed at the floor in front of him. He looked worried and this intrigued me enough that I actually forgot where I was for a moment. When he looked up and straight at me, I didn't look away fast enough. His green eyes locked on mine, then frown on his face turned into a warm half smile that could literally give me a heart attack if I weren't on my new meds.

"You're in Warner's class with me," he stated. It

wasn't a question. There was no way I could mistake sitting next to him for an hour a day for the past four months.

I nodded, tightening my grip on the back of my hospital gown and hoping he didn't look down at my feet. My mom didn't bother painting my toenails while I was in a coma. It didn't seem important at the time.

He stopped just a couple of feet away, close enough for me to smell the warm, fresh scent of his black T-shirt, which bore the logo of a band I'd never heard of. God, why was he smiling at me like that?

"I heard you were in the hospital."

"You did?" I replied, my voice a bit shrill as I wondered what exactly he heard and who he heard it from. He probably thought I was totally lame and sickly.

"Yeah, I asked about you and Ewan said you were in the hospital for your heart."

"You asked about me?"

"What's wrong with your heart?"

I looked up into his gorgeous green eyes and tried not to collapse right there. I managed to hold it together long enough to tell him about my reaction to the old meds and to find out why he was in the hospital that day. His dad also had liver problems, caused by something totally different. In the ten minutes we spoke, I saw something in his eyes I'd never seen in Mr. Warner's class.

Hope.

I type up my reply and hold my breath as I hit send.

From: abigailjensen13@gmail.com
To: ceverett0115@gmail.com
Subject: Re: homework

134-139 and 156-158. 156-158 is the practice test and it's hard. You should get started on that or you'll be up all night. ;-)

My stomach flutters as I wait for his response. The moment my email dings, my fingers race to open the new message.

From: ceverett0115@gmail.com
To: abigailjensen13@gmail.com
Subject: Re: homework

do you think warner will go easy on me if I tell him I couldn't finish 'cause I was too busy emailing my future girlfriend?

Just a few simple, corny words and everything has changed. Just a few words and I have… hope.

CHAPTER SIX

Brian

A PANG OF GUILT twists inside my chest when I open the safe-deposit box. Between the holidays and three weeks standing vigil at Abby's bedside in the hospital, we never made it here to deposit the pictures of Abby before Christmas, as per our agreement with the Knights. I'd like to leave a note of apology for not having the updated photos deposited in time, but Lynette and I both agreed we shouldn't communicate with them until we're ready for them to meet Abby. Besides, if we tell them Abby was in the hospital, it will just worry them unnecessarily. She's fine now. For the most part.

I carry the metal box to the chair in the back of the

room and set it down on the plastic seat. Reaching into my coat pocket, I pull out a stack of pictures of Abby I had developed yesterday during a trip to the drugstore. I open the small plastic case hanging from my keychain and lift out the memory card. I remove the stack of pictures and the memory card the Knights left for us and replace them with the ones I brought with me. Then I tuck the Knights' photos and memory card into my coat pocket and heave a deep sigh.

I've been doing this every year since Abby was a toddler and I've never felt like I was doing anything wrong, until today. I feel like a damn thief, stealing my daughter's memories and tucking them away in a box inside my closet until a time when *I* determine she's ready to experience them.

When they brought Abby out of the hospital room more than thirteen years ago, all I wanted to do was hold her in my arms. Then they told us she hadn't scored a two on the five-minute Apgar test. Her heart rate was slower than 100 beats per minute. They told us they would check her again at ten minutes post-birth. But they never did. They rushed her into surgery three minutes later.

I've recalled that day with such shame for thirteen years. My first reaction to Abby's eight-minute-old body being wheeled away into a surgical suite was to make sure the nurses knew that the birth mother was not to be made aware of Abby's problems. In my mind, she was *my* baby and bringing Claire into the situation would only complicate matters. I'd read about "failed adoptions" where the biological mother changed her mind after giving birth. Of course, Claire found out about Abby's heart four months later when Chris Knight's lawyer contacted us.

But not a single day went by when I didn't wonder what would have happened if we had told Claire about Abby's heart right when she was born. Would she have changed her mind about the adoption? Or would she have given us some critical piece of information that could have helped Abby? Would Claire have taken better care of Abby's heart?

I can't even fathom the answers to these questions anymore. Abby is *my* baby. She always will be, whether or not we introduce her to Claire and Chris.

CHAPTER SEVEN

Three days before

THE MALL PARKING LOT is packed, as usual, but Caleb manages to eke out a parking space near the entrance to the food court. He pulls his convertible 1967 Plymouth Barracuda into the space and kills the engine, but he doesn't move.

"Put up the top. It's supposed to rain," I say, scooping my purse off the floor by my feet.

Caleb grabs my hand before I can exit the car. "Wait. We need to talk."

I sigh and drop my purse onto my lap. "I'm fine, okay? I don't want to talk about my birthday anymore."

Caleb has been trying to make me talk about my

upcoming eighteenth birthday for the past two months, but I'm not going to do it. In three days, I will be eighteen years old when I wake up. Then, and only then, will I decide whether or not I'm going to visit the safe-deposit box in Raleigh. I know myself. If I try to make that decision now, it will be too difficult to change my mind later.

"It's not about your birthday, Abby. Can we please talk? I'm tired of you blowing me off."

I glare at him in confusion. "I have not been blowing you off."

He pulls my hand into his lap. "I know. I'm sorry. I'm just really nervous about this."

"Nervous about what? You're scaring me, Caleb."

He looks into my eyes. "I don't want to scare you. I just want to talk to you. About something very important."

Holy crap. I don't think Caleb would break up with me, but I have seen Jodi Weathers trying to flirt with him after fourth period. What the hell does he want to talk to me about?

He takes my hand in both of his and mine disappears as he pulls it to his chest. "Abby, baby, I'm pregnant."

I wrench my hand away and punch his shoulder.

"You asshole! I thought you were gonna break up with me."

He laughs as he grabs my hand and pulls me toward him. "Baby, don't get mad. I thought you would take the news better than this." I laugh as he takes me in his arms and pretends to cry on my shoulder. "Please don't make me raise this baby alone."

"Shut up, jerk."

He chuckles and plants a loud kiss on my cheek before he lets me go. "It's not my fault you can't remember April Fool's Day."

"I remembered!" I insist, grabbing my purse and throwing the car door open. "I was just playing along."

"You're a bad liar, sunshine."

He puts up the top on the convertible, then we head for the food court. I hate the food court, but I'll do anything to get away from my house right now. Every time I look into my mother's face, I see the silent plea for me to not visit that safe-deposit box on Friday. She doesn't realize that her need to keep me from knowing my birth parents only makes me want to know them even more. I mean, what the hell is she hiding? What am I going to find in that safe-deposit box?

I keep expecting I'm going to find my birth mother is a drug addict and my father works at McDonald's or something similar. But the way my mom seems intent on keeping their identities a secret only makes me wonder if maybe my biological parents aren't strung-out losers. Maybe they're politicians or movie stars. It's possible.

Anyway, it doesn't matter. All that matters is I'm not going to decide until Friday. On Friday, I'll know what to do. Today, I'm too freaked out about my mom's shifty behavior and my boyfriend's fake pregnancy.

Caleb and I grab some Chinese food then walk around for about ten minutes before someone vacates their table and we swoop in to take it. Caleb wipes the table down while I hold our tray, then we sit down to enjoy our orange chicken.

"Do you want to know what I'm getting you for your birthday?" he asks, then he wraps his lips around his straw and takes a long pull of his soda.

The tattoo on the outer edge of his forearm always makes me smile. Caleb had a few tattoos when we first got together four and a half years ago, but his arms are pretty much covered in them now. The tattoo on the outside of his forearm is very simple, yet it's definitely my favorite. It's half of a heart. I'm supposed to get the other half tattooed on my arm when I'm eighteen. That way, when we hold hands, our hearts will be whole.

There's no way my parents would let me get a tattoo before my eighteenth birthday, so I haven't even bothered asking. I'm actually surprised they're allowing me to visit the safe-deposit box on Friday, should I choose to do so. It's *their* box. They don't have to show me anything. They could tell me to go to the county courthouse if I want to find out who my parents are. But they haven't. They've agreed to give me the key on my birthday, whether I want it or not.

"Why would I want to know what you're getting me for my birthday? That would totally ruin the surprise."

"Well, being surprised is not always a good thing. Look at how you reacted to my pregnancy."

I roll my eyes and take a drink of soda. "Do you want to tell me what you got me for my birthday?"

He smiles and I don't even have to know the answer to that question. Caleb is so terrible at keeping secrets.

Caleb PULLS THE 'Cuda into the parking lot of Eastgate Park at ten p.m. and I smile at his knack for remembering small details. He remembers where I was when I collapsed on the soccer field and was rushed to the hospital almost five years ago. He insists God was looking out for me that day. I wish I could feel as certain about that as he is.

We get out of the car and he immediately heads for the trunk. "It's in here."

"We were driving around with my present in your trunk this whole time?"

"Yep. And it's not even wrapped."

He pops the trunk open as I arrive at the back of the car. The moment I see it, my eyes begin to tear up and my throat constricts painfully.

"You got it?"

He reaches into the trunk and gently lifts the guitar out. "I got it months ago," he says, holding out the Gibson Hummingbird acoustic-electric guitar I've been coveting for two years. "I asked the guy to keep it in the window in case you came back to look at it, as you always do."

"You can't afford this."

He slings the strap over my shoulders. "Yes, I can. The estate lawyer sent me a check a few months ago."

The tears come faster at this news. Caleb's father passed away last year and he's been waiting for the estate lawyer who handled his father's will to disburse the inheritance. He told me he was going to get the meager inheritance on his eighteenth birthday in January. But when January came and went without any news from Caleb, I was too afraid to bring it up.

"I can't accept this. This is a $4,000 guitar. That's almost half your inheritance."

"That money means nothing to me if I can't use it on the only family I have left in this world."

My fingers fall on the smooth body of the guitar and a chill passes through me. Caleb is the one who made me test out the guitar in the store two years ago. I haven't been able to stop thinking about it since. The sound was so beautiful and resonant it made me cry. But to hold it in my hands... to carry it home with me and call it my own... that's beyond a dream come true. It's a miracle.

"Caleb, I'll always be your family. You don't need to give me this."

"It's not a bribe." He takes my face in his hands and kisses my forehead. "I just want to see you smile."

I pull up the neck of my T-shirt and wipe the tears from my face. "Okay, I'll keep it. But only if you let me play a lullaby for you and the baby."

He scrunches his eyebrows together and smiles. "Of course," he replies, rubbing his belly. "Let's go lie under the stars. You, me, Junior, and—" His mouth drops open. "What are you gonna name the guitar?"

I shrug. "I hadn't thought of that. What do you think I should name it?"

He slams the trunk closed then wraps his arm around my shoulder as we walk toward the soccer field. "How about Caleb's Love Slave or 'Cuda Monster?"

I shake my head. "Terrible. How about… Blackbird?"

Caleb is silent as we trudge through the damp grass. I begin to wonder if he didn't hear me, then he finally speaks. "You mean, like, a blackbird with broken wings?"

I stop walking and look up at him. "No. Like a blackbird who's learning to fly."

He smiles and nods toward the field for us to keep going. "I like that better."

We find a nice flat patch of grass and Caleb lays his hoodie on the ground for us to sit down. The hoodie isn't big enough for both of us to sit on while I'm sitting cross-legged with the guitar in my lap. So we decide it's okay to get a little wet and we lie back to gaze at the stars.

I feel around the frets until my fingers are in the correct position, then I begin plucking the strings, playing one of the first songs Caleb ever sang for me four and a half years ago: "You're My Best Friend" by Queen.

I spend a whole hour playing songs for Caleb, pretending I can't feel my phone vibrating in my pocket. But when his phone starts ringing, I know it's time for me to head home. It's Tuesday and my parents prefer to have me back before midnight on school nights.

I sit up and remove the guitar strap from around my neck as Caleb answers the call and immediately passes me the phone. "I'll be home in twenty minutes," I say, not bothering to say *hello* or *who is this?*

"You should have been home twenty minutes ago," my mom replies.

"It's only 11:30. I don't have to be home until midnight."

"That doesn't mean you have to stay out until midnight every night of the week, Abby. Get home."

She hangs up before I can argue. I hand Caleb the phone and the guitar so I can stand up. He slings the guitar strap over his neck and begins playing an upbeat variation on "Blackbird" as we head back to the car. Caleb can probably play guitar better than I can, but he prefers drums. So he has a tendency to smack the guitar while he plays. I usually love it, but I'll admit I'm a little nervous as I watch him banging on my new instrument.

"Dance, Abby. Dance like nobody's watching."

I shake my head and smile. Caleb once told me how much he hated corny catchphrases because they're never as meaningful as the words that are unrehearsed and spoken from the heart. Then, a few weeks later, he found a diary my mom gave me when I was ten and the quote on the cover read "Dance like nobody's watching." Ever since then, it's become our little inside joke. He knows it's the one phrase that will always make me smile.

We stand next to the trunk of the car as he finishes the song. When he's done, I clap and he takes a bow, then he carefully places the guitar back in the trunk.

I gaze at it longingly. "Can you hold on to it for me? I don't want my parents to ask me about it and find out how much it cost. We'll let them find out after we move in together."

He smiles as he slams the trunk shut. "Whatever you say."

"Are you mad?"

"What? Of course not."

He bends his knees a bit so he can wrap his arms around my waist and lift me up. I coil my arms around his neck and lay my head on his sturdy shoulder. He plants a soft kiss on my neck and I sigh.

"Anything that makes it easier for us to be together is fine by me," he whispers against my skin.

I tighten my arms around his neck so I can lift my legs and wrap them around his hips. He chuckles as he turns me around and sets me down on top of the trunk. I tilt my head back and he swallows hard as I gaze into his emerald eyes.

"I love you, my little blackbird. You should know by now that I'll never say no to you."

I squeeze my legs tighter around him to bring him closer and I'm not surprised when I feel a slight bulge in his jeans. "Kiss me before midnight or I'll turn into a real blackbird."

"As you wish."

His mouth falls gently over mine and I run my fingers through the soft hair on the back of his head.

He moans into my mouth and I smile as I kiss him harder. He loves when I run my fingers through his hair.

"Slow down, sunshine."

I sigh as I push him away. "Let's go."

"Hey, don't get mad. I'm just trying to keep you from getting too excited."

"Yeah, yeah. I've heard it a million times. Just take me home."

I open the passenger door and he slams it shut before I can get inside. "I know you've heard it before, but can you please not make me feel like a total asshole for trying to keep you safe?"

"I'm not going to have a heart attack from kissing you!"

"I know that, Abby. But there are things I want to do with you... *to* you, and I don't know how your body will react. You can't expect me to not be afraid."

I lean back against the side of the car and he lays his hands flat on the glass, boxing me in. "Things you want to do *to* me?"

He chuckles as he leans in and lays a tender kiss on my jaw. "Yes. I want to..."

My hands reach forward. Finding his solid chest, I grab fistfuls of his T-shirt. "You want to *what?*"

His lips travel from my jaw up to my ear. "I want to taste you."

He traces his tongue along the edge of my earlobe and I tighten my grip on his shirt so I don't collapse. "Okay, okay, that's enough."

He pulls his head back to look me in the eye. "Are you okay?"

I nod quickly. "Yes, but I have to go home."

He smiles and kisses my temple. "Pretty soon we'll be at NC State and we'll be going home together."

I sigh as I kiss him on the cheek. "I can't wait for the summer to be over."

CHAPTER EIGHT

Lynette

The day of
Abby's eighteenth birthday

I LOCK THE BEDROOM door and head straight for the closet. Today is the day I've been dreading for eighteen years. I wish I had it in me to throw away that box of photos. But, as much as I fear not measuring up to Abby's birth parents, I have a greater fear of watching Abby live the rest of her life feeling broken and betrayed by me.

I slide the closet door open and look up at the shoebox on the shelf. It's a large box. Brian wears a size fourteen. Despite his size, Brian has the most gentle heart of anyone I've ever known. I know his need to share these photos with Abby is largely inspired by guilt.

Brian was badly electrocuted after seven months at his job as an electrician. He was just nineteen years old and he was told by his doctor to get fertility testing when he was twenty-three. He didn't meet me until he was twenty-five and I was twenty-one. We got married three years later and immediately began trying for a child. After five months with no success, I was baffled.

I'd had an abortion my sophomore year in college, and I began to wonder if the abortion had damaged me. Then, Brian remembered his doctor had recommended fertility testing to him almost ten years earlier. It was a huge blow to his ego. He was twenty-eight years old and unable to father his own children. It was devastating to both of us, but he took it especially hard. He even offered to divorce me so that I could be with someone who wasn't defective. In the end, we decided to adopt.

It took four years, $67,000, and countless tears for us to become parents. So, yes, it was extremely disheartening and terrifying when Abby was just four months old and we were contacted by Chris Knight's lawyer. This was the man whose music I listened to while cooking dinner, and he was asking to be a part of my daughter's life.

At first, I didn't see how it couldn't be a good

thing for Abby. It was Brian who was looking into the future and seeing all the times Abby would go running to the Knights, the beautiful, rich couple who would probably never feel the need to discipline Abby. They'd leave that part to us, so they could remain the good guys. At least, this is how Brian saw the future if we agreed to an open adoption. I think he was right.

I slide the box off the shelf and I'm surprised by how heavy it is. Brian is the one in charge of taking the pictures out of the safe-deposit box and putting them in this box. I did have a slight crush on Chris Knight eighteen years ago, so I thought it would be best if Brian handled this part. Though, I never told him why. Even eighteen years later, I'm still not sure how I'll feel when I see these pictures. But I need to look at them before Abby does. I need to make sure there are no objectionable photos in here.

I place the box in the master bathroom, then I unlock the master bedroom door. Racing back to the bathroom, I lock the door behind me. I turn the cold water on in the shower, then I sit on the toilet and place the box in my lap. Abby's in the bathroom down the hall, getting ready to go to school. This is my only opportunity to do this before Brian leaves for work.

I lift the lid on the box and the first photo is of

Claire Knight holding Abby in that conference room more than seventeen years ago. I didn't know they had taken photos of Abby while they were in there. I'm not sure how I feel about that.

I take a few breaths to calm myself, then I flip to the next photo in the stack. My heart races when I see another picture from that meeting in the conference room, but this one is with Abby and Chris. They're both smiling as she reaches for his mouth. She has his brown eyes, the feature of her appearance that made her question why she doesn't look like Brian or me.

I set the pictures back in the box and replace the lid. I can't do this. Brian will have to return the photos to the safe-deposit box without me. I don't have the strength to look through these hundreds of pictures while suffering such feelings of inadequacy.

We'll never be as young or wealthy or good looking as the Knights. And I know it's ridiculous to envy a woman who obviously has emotional issues after dealing with the suicide of her mother, but I do. I envy Claire. I don't know how she got Chris to forgive her after she gave Abigail up for adoption without his knowledge. All I know is that this adoption nearly broke Brian and me more times than I can count. I won't allow a box of photos to deliver the final blow.

Abby

AMY RIDES HOME with Caleb and me after school. An April storm swooped in while we were in third period. The smell of the rain and the sound of the drops tapping on the vinyl convertible top is soothing after a long day of fake smiles. Amy and Caleb are the only people who know about the significance of today's date. Everyone at school was wishing me a happy eighteenth birthday, completely oblivious as to how unhappy today actually is.

I haven't told Caleb or Amy, but I've already made my decision about opening the safe-deposit box.

Caleb pulls into the driveway, next to my dad's silver pickup truck, and turns off the engine. The silence that follows brings a smile to my face. They're both waiting for direction from me.

"Let's go. I'm sure my mom is pacing the living room, waiting for me to walk through the front door."

Caleb laughs, but Amy shakes her head. Her wavy brown hair is damp at the ends from the rain and the light freckles on her nose are showing through her makeup, but she still looks great. My makeup is probably all gone.

"Is your mom going to freak out?"

I push the passenger door open and a few raindrops fall on my arm. "Amy, this is my mom. Of course she's going to freak out… on the inside. On the outside, she'll pretend like everything is okay."

Caleb grabs my shoulder as we stroll up the front walk, then he gives it a soft squeeze. "Whatever you choose is the right choice. Don't let anyone make you believe otherwise."

I smile and, for some reason, the $4,000 guitar lying in his trunk comes to mind. Of course Caleb thinks that whatever I choose is the right choice. He thinks I'm so special I actually deserve a $4,000 guitar. I could probably run away tonight and Caleb would tell me I made the right choice. Of course, if I ran away tonight I'd probably end up spending the night with Caleb at the apartment he shares with his twenty-three-year-old roommate. So that's a bit obvious.

"Is your dad supposed to be home right now?" Amy asks as I reach for the doorknob.

"No, he probably left work early. It's a big day for them, too." Pushing open the front door, I'm a bit surprised to find my dad standing in the foyer, as if he were waiting for me. "Hey, Dad."

He clears his throat and smiles. "I know I wished you a happy birthday this morning, but I'm going to do it again." He extends his right hand forward and I see the gold key lying flat in his palm. "Happy birthday, sweetheart. This is yours now."

I draw in a few deep breaths, then I reach forward and take the key from his hand. I curl my fist around the sharp metal, squeezing as it digs into the soft flesh of my palm. Looking up into my father's blue eyes, the barely disguised grimace crinkling the skin around the corners, I tuck the key into the front pocket of my jeans.

"I'm not going today," I say, smiling so he doesn't think this was a difficult decision to make. "I don't know if I ever will, but thank you for trusting me to make the decision on my own. I love you, Dad."

I wrap my arms around his thick waist and he squeezes my shoulders so tight it hurts. "I've always trusted you, sweetheart. I know you'll make the right decision for you."

"What's going on?"

My mom's voice is soft and laced with worry, but it still grates on my nerves. I love my mom, but her inability to trust that I would make the right decision has broken something between us. I don't know if I'll ever hear her speak and hear the same voice that sang me to sleep every night until I was eight years old.

"I'm not going," I say, letting go of my dad.

Her eyebrows knit together, but there's a spark of hope in her eyes and a slight curl to her lips. "Why not?"

I blink a few times to hold back the tears. "Because I'm afraid of hurting you."

"What? That's silly."

"No, it's not. I can see how much you want me to leave that part of me in the past. Even if you don't say it, I can see it in your eyes."

"I'm sorry, Abby. I just—"

"No, you don't have to explain, Mom. I understand." I sniff loudly as I wipe the tears from my face. "You don't want to lose me. And I'm lucky to have you. I know that… I don't want to lose you either."

She shakes her head and takes my face in her hands. "Oh, honey. You're not going to lose me. You'll never lose me." She kisses my forehead and tucks my hair behind my ear. "Yes, I'm afraid of what this will do to our family going forward, but it's natural. We fought so hard for you, Abby. I just want to protect you. I want to protect this family."

"From what?"

She presses her lips together as she considers this question. "I don't know. But please don't let my fear influence you. This is your decision, honey. Your father and I will support you no matter what you choose to do."

I nod and she takes me into her arms. I allow myself to cry on her shoulder for a moment, before I excuse myself to my bedroom with Caleb and Amy. Closing the door behind us, I immediately take a seat on my bed while Amy sits at my desk and Caleb sits next to me.

"She's hiding something from me," I say as Caleb grabs my hand.

"Our parents probably hide more things from us than we do from them," Amy replies, opening up my laptop. "Do you want me to respond to all your birthday greetings on Facebook?"

"Yes, please."

"Not the ones from guys," Caleb adds, and I shove him. "Are you sure you don't want to see what's inside that box?"

I nod quickly. "I'm not ready. I'm actually glad my

mom made me wait. I don't know if I'll ever be ready to face the people who gave me away."

"What if they had no choice?" Amy says.

"No choice? In what kind of world would they have *no* choice? Of course they had a choice. Maybe it was a difficult one, but it was still the choice they made. Why do I even want to meet someone who didn't want me? My parents want me. They've always wanted me and now I'm going to risk hurting them just to satisfy my curiosity? It doesn't make sense."

"You'll know when you're ready," Amy says, an automatic response as she scrolls through my Facebook profile and responds to hundreds of birthday wishes.

"That's bullshit."

I look up at Caleb and he's staring straight at me. "What?"

"That's bullshit," he repeats. "You're not going to hurt your parents. And you know that."

I try to let go of his hand, but he tightens his grip. "You don't know what you're talking about."

"I know better than you do. I had a mother who didn't want me. *Really* didn't want me. But you... you don't know what your birth parents felt about you and I think that's what scares you the most. Not knowing."

The soft tapping of Amy's fingers on the keyboard of my laptop stops. I bite my lip as I try to deny that what Caleb just said is true, but I can't. He's right. I'm not afraid of hurting my parents. I'm afraid of hurting me.

CHAPTER NINE

Two months after

I KNOW THAT, technically, I'm doing nothing wrong.
I'm an adult. I have the right to decide where I want to
spend the night. But lying to my parents always makes
me anxious. Still, I don't think it's the lie that's got me
so worked up. I'm afraid to spend the night with
Caleb.

I shouldn't be afraid of spending the night with
him. We're not going to have sex. At least, I don't
think we are.

"So Amy is going to keep her ringer on all night in
case they call, right?" Caleb asks as we drive toward the
apartment he shares with his roommate, Greg Lawson.

I've hung out with Greg plenty of times and he's

agreed to spend the night at his girlfriend's house to give us some privacy. But I can't help but feel weird about this whole thing. Even knowing that this will be our apartment soon.

Greg graduated from UNC Chapel Hill two years ago. He was the only person Caleb found who was willing to take a chance on a seventeen-year-old roommate after Caleb's dad died last year. Caleb absolutely did not want to get placed in foster care at his age. He asked for more hours at the tire shop where he works to bring in some more cash, and he's been living with Greg ever since. Until Greg gets married and moves out in July. Then, Caleb and I have agreed we'll take over the lease.

Caleb and I are going to live together.

It feels surreal as he turns left off Stanhope, into College Crest. College Crest is a neighborhood just east of NC State and Meredith College, mostly inhabited by college-age residents. Greg took over the lease on this apartment when his friend from NC State moved to Seattle after graduation. Two years on, and now Caleb and I will be assuming the lease. It's hard to find a vacant apartment in College Crest.

"Yes, Amy is going to keep her phone on and she's going to answer," I reply, sliding my right hand between the seat and the passenger door to hide it as I wiggle my fingers. I run the fingers of my left hand through my hair to disguise the same action. I don't want Caleb to know how terrified I am right now.

He reaches across and grabs my hand out of my hair as he turns into the parking lot on Stanhope. "Are you panicking?"

He rubs his thumb over the top of my hand and I close my eyes as I draw in a large breath.

"A little."

He pulls his car into an empty space near the back of the lot, but he doesn't turn off the engine. "We don't have to do this. I'll take you home right now and you can decide what you want to do later… Or now. You can tell me right now if you don't want to live here. I'll find another roommate… Or I'll give you this apartment and find another place."

"Caleb, stop. We've discussed this. I'm not taking this apartment without you, and I'm not going to try to find another roommate. No one else will understand me the way you do." I look down at his hand in mine and smile. "I'm going to live with you. Nothing else makes sense." I look up and he's not smiling. "But that doesn't mean I'm not really nervous about tonight."

"Abby, you don't have to be nervous. I'll sleep in

Greg's room and you can sleep in mine. It will be like sleeping in your own bed, only it'll smell much better."

I shake my head as I reach for the door handle. "You always know what to say to make me feel *so* much better."

We enter the apartment and, after he drops my backpack on top of the kitchen table, Caleb heads straight for the refrigerator. "I stocked up on Cheerwine for you," he calls to me as I take a seat on the navy-blue sofa where Caleb and I have made out a thousand times.

He comes out of the kitchen with a can of Cheerwine, my favorite cherry soda, and a bottle of drinkable yogurt for himself. Caleb is addicted to drinkable yogurt, and not the fruity kind. He drinks the plain stuff, which I find disgusting. But he claims it gives him super powers.

He sits next to me, handing me the soda and offering me a sip of his yogurt. He smiles when I shake my head. "You're missing out." He grabs the TV remote off the coffee table and turns on the DVR. "I even recorded your favorite show," he says, scrolling through a long list of episodes of Congressional Chronicle on C-Span.

I open my Cheerwine and take my shoes off so I

can curl my feet up on the sofa. "You really are the perfect roommate."

He puts on a romantic comedy movie he obviously recorded for me, then he sets the remote down on the table. "Tonight is your night, angel-face."

"Angel-face?"

He guzzles the last drops of yogurt and places the empty bottle on the table. "Do you prefer sunshine?"

I take a large gulp of soda and place the can on the table, then I lie back with my head in Caleb's lap. "Let's mix it up. How about… turtledove?"

"Turtledove it is."

He runs his fingers through my hair as we watch the movie and I don't notice I've fallen asleep until I wake up in Caleb's arms as he carries me to his bedroom.

"I can walk," I mutter groggily.

"It's fine. This totally makes up for the fact that I didn't get to work out today."

He lays me down on the bed and I'm fully awake now. "I have to get ready for bed," I say, sitting up immediately.

Caleb holds up his hand to stop me. "I'll get your stuff."

He returns a moment later with my backpack. "I

know you take a shower before you go to bed. I'll just go… out there until you're done."

"Wait."

He looks at me with that hopeful look in his eyes and my entire body is buzzing with anxiety. "Can you turn on the water in the shower for me?"

He smiles and nods for me to follow him. We enter the small bathroom and the first thing I think is that it desperately needs some new decor. The plastic shower curtain is covered in squiggly blue lines that are meant to resemble waves. But in between each line, there's nothing. It's just clear plastic. And the shower curtain liner behind it is also clear. Not very private.

I put down the toilet seat and the lid and Caleb smiles. "I knew I forgot something. Damn toilet seat gets me every time."

The nice thing about being an only child is that I've never had to share my bathroom. Our small three-bedroom, two-bath house in Raleigh is just big enough for our family. My dad never goes in my bathroom, so I've never had the pleasure of accidentally sitting down on a toilet while the seat is still up. But every time I've visited Caleb's apartment over the past ten months, I always find the toilet seat up. It's not a big deal, but it's one of those classic reminders of the things that happen when a male and female share a living space.

"Just don't let it happen again, buttercup," I reply, setting my backpack on the closed lid of the toilet as Caleb squeezes in next to me and pushes the shower curtain open.

"Turn it to the left to turn it on," he says, turning on the water in the shower. "Wait a little while until it gets hot, then turn it back to the right if you want it cooler or to the left if you want it hotter. But be careful, it gets really hot. Greg rigged the water heater to go full throttle."

"Full throttle?" I say, pulling my shampoo, conditioner, and body wash out of my backpack. "I'm going to make sure to tell my parents we went full throttle in the shower."

He spins around and his eyes are wide with surprise. "Turtledove, I'm shocked."

I laugh as I pull my pajamas out of my backpack and set them down on the bathroom counter. "Get out."

After a long shower, my muscles are warm and relaxed. I enter Caleb's bedroom and find the lamp on, but he's not here. I set my backpack on the floor and head for the living room. He's laid out on the sofa watching a political satire show on the comedy channel. He watches me as I approach, then I lie down on top of him, nuzzling my head into the crook of his neck.

"You smell like sunshine," he whispers, planting a soft kiss on the top of my head.

"We can do this, right?"

He knows I'm referring to living together, so he doesn't skip a beat with his reply. "We can do anything you want."

I lie still for a moment, listening to the beat of his heart beneath me. "I want to go to sleep… with you… roomie."

After Caleb showers and we settle into his freshly laundered sheets, I sneak back into his nook and he holds me until I fall asleep. When I wake seven hours later, I'm surprised to find neither of us has changed positions. My face is still mashed against his neck and his hand is still wrapped loosely around my shoulders. It's almost as if God is trying to tell us something. *"See, Abby. You're still you and Caleb is still Caleb. Everything is going to be just fine."*

WE PICK UP AMY at nine a.m., as planned, then we

have breakfast at McDonald's before we head back to my house. Caleb and I have breakfast on Saturdays quite often, and he drives me everywhere, so my mom won't suspect anything when we show up in his car. They won't know that Caleb and I just did a trial run on our soon-to-be new living situation and everything went great. They won't know that I'm about to say good-bye.

My dad is in the backyard, the sound of the hedge trimmer buzzing. My mom is in the kitchen doing the breakfast dishes. Caleb, Amy, and I enter and I grab a towel to dry the dishes that are already in the rack. I dry the first plate then hand it to Caleb for him to put away.

"What are you doing today, Mom?"

She casts me that suspicious sideways glance that tells me she knows I'm up to something. "I'm going to lunch with your Aunt Maddie. What are you three doing?"

Amy opens the refrigerator and grabs the pitcher of cold water. I hand her a glass tumbler I just dried and she heads to the dining table with the glass and the entire pitcher of water.

"We're thinking of going to Jockey's Ridge," I reply, taking the clean skillet from my mom.

"Jockey's Ridge again? You graduated eight days ago and you're already repeating your summer outings. Why don't you all go to the movies or something?"

"That's a great idea!" I say as I hang the skillet up on the pot rack above the tiny kitchen island. "But... I have something I need to talk to you about first. Well, Caleb and I have something we need to talk to you about."

My mom finishes drying off her hands on a clean towel then turns around. "What do you have to talk to me about?"

"We kind of wanted to talk to you and Dad."

She looks at me like I'm crazy. "Abigail, is this something serious? What is going on here?"

"I'm not pregnant or anything, if that's what you're thinking."

She lets out a huge sigh and shakes her head. "Jesus, Abby. You scared the heck out of me. Your dad will be done soon."

We all retire to the living room to watch some TV while we wait for my dad. My mom puts on the Animal Planet and I know Caleb is dying to make a smart comment. Every time we sit down to watch TV with my mom, she always puts on the Animal Planet. It's almost as if she thinks this is the only safe channel to watch with us. Caleb thought he was so clever when he bought my mom an Animal Planet Explorer lifetime membership for her last birthday.

My dad walks in through the front door about twenty minutes later. My leg bounces impatiently as I wait for him to wash his hands and find us in the living room. When he comes out of the kitchen, he chuckles when he sees us all sitting down together and staring straight at him.

"Is this some kind of meeting of the minds? How'd it go last night, sweetheart?"

"It was great!" I reply quickly, shooting a glance at Amy.

"It was awesome, Mr. Jensen," Amy begins. "We went for some fro-yo, then we watched pay-per-view porn all night."

"Amy!" my mom shrieks while Caleb and I laugh.

"Oh, sorry. Was I not supposed to tell them about that?" Amy asks with a smile.

I can always count on her to completely erase any doubt that we were together. Though, according to Amy, my parents never called her all night. My mom did call me around ten o'clock to make sure I was okay and that I'd taken my nightly meds. But other than that, my sleepover with Caleb went off without a hitch.

It's almost frightening how easy it is to lie to my parents. Maybe I can lie to them about living off-campus with Caleb.

No, I could never pull that off. The stress alone would kill me.

And speaking of stress, here goes nothing.

"Mom, Dad. Caleb and I are going to share an apartment off-campus this fall."

"What?" my mom and dad bellow.

"That is not even funny, Abby," my mom says, her mouth hanging open as she waits for me to tell her this is a joke.

"Your mom's right," my dad agrees. "The porn joke was funny, but this is not."

"It's not a joke!" I shout as I push up from the sofa. "I'm eighteen years old. I'm allowed to live with whomever I choose and I want to live with Caleb. He knows me better than anyone. He knows when I'm stressed. He knows when I need to take my meds. He knows how to take care of me better than any random roommate ever will." I look at Caleb and he has his head down, but I can see a shadow of a smile on his lips. "And we love each other."

"Was this your idea?" my dad roars.

Caleb raises his head and I'm pleased to find he

looks more surprised than scared. "No, sir. This was not my idea, but Abby's right. I can take care of her better than anyone. I'd rather have her with me where I know she's safe."

My dad narrows his eyes and nods his head. "Where she's safe? Sure, that's exactly why you want to live with her. Do you two really think I'm that stupid?"

Caleb and my mom stand from the sofa at the same time, but I speak first. "We don't think you're stupid, Dad. We thought you'd be more understanding."

"You thought I'd understand that my eighteen-year-old daughter and her eighteen-year-old boyfriend want to live together?" His glare is seething with a rage I've never seen on my father. "You thought I'd understand that you seem determined to repeat your parents' mistakes?"

The room is so quiet after my father speaks these words, I can almost hear the tears welling up in my eyes. Everyone in this room knows what "parents" my father is referring to. And this is the first clue about their story that I've ever been given. And it only saddens me more that he used this piece of information to hurt me.

"How could you say that to me?" I whisper.

"Abby, you don't know what you're proposing. This is bigger than just picking a roommate," my mom says, reaching for my arm, but I push her away. "Your father's right. Accidents happen and you're not physically or emotionally prepared to deal with something like that. You two need to finish college first before you start a life together."

"I'm not emotionally prepared? I'm too fragile?" I shake my head. "You two don't know me at all. Maybe I am more like my other parents."

"Your father didn't mean that."

I grab Caleb's hand and pull him toward the front door as Amy follows behind us. "That's okay, because I think it's time for me to find out for myself."

CHAPTER TEN

Caleb

I CARRY THE STACK of photos for Abby as we cross the bank parking lot toward the 'Cuda. Her hands were shaking while we were inside that vault and the last thing I need is for her to drop the pictures in the middle of the parking lot and get hit by a car as she tries to pick them up. Yeah, I know it sounds totally far-fetched. But I'm in charge of keeping Abby safe now. And I can't rule out the possibility of her being mowed down by a car, now that every possible thing that could go wrong today has gone wrong.

I knew her dad and mom wouldn't take the news about Abby and me moving in together well, but I didn't expect them to deliver such a low blow. Though

I know her father said what he said out of desperation, it doesn't excuse the fact that he hurt her. If he weren't her father, I would have punched him in the throat. But he *is* Abby's father. The only father she's ever known, until today. And he's just scared of losing her.

I open the passenger door for Abby and she slides in. I hand her the stack of photos, then I round the back of the car and get inside. We sit in silence for a moment as she stares at the picture on the top of the stack.

I can't fucking believe Chris Knight is Abby's dad. If we hadn't seen their family portrait first, I might have believed it was just a picture her birth parents had snapped of a celebrity holding Abby. But we did see that family photo. And the only teenage girl in that picture had brown hair. The baby in that picture with Chris Knight is clearly Abby with her golden blonde hair and wide brown eyes. I've seen a million baby pictures of Abby, but this one definitely puts the others in perspective.

She moves the photo on top to the bottom of the stack and the next picture is of the brown-haired girl from the family photo. She's obviously younger in this one, about eight or nine years old. She's clutching a picture to her chest. It's a photo of Abby I've seen before. This one seems to be too much for her. She turns the entire stack of photos over so they're facedown in her lap.

"I have a sister," she whispers.

"And a couple of brothers," I say. "The youngest one looks like you, doesn't he?"

She looks up, her brow furrowed. "You think so?"

Her fair skin is glistening with tears. *How could her parents keep this from her for so long?* She could have used a sister and brother with everything she's been through. Then a slightly selfish thought crosses my mind. If she'd had siblings, would Abby and I still be this close?

I reach for the photos in her lap and she watches as I take them. It takes me a second to find the family portrait in the bottom of the stack and I hold it up between us so we can both look at it.

"Look. He has the same blonde hair and brown eyes as you."

She stares at the picture for a while before she takes it in her hand to examine it up close. "He does." Her silent tears turn into a soft whimpering cry. "These are my parents... This is the family I never knew I had."

I quickly sift through the photos, searching for the one of the little girl holding Abby's picture. "But it looks like they knew about you," I say, holding it up for her, "and you never left their thoughts." Her shoulders tremble as they curl inward, and she clutches her fist to her chest. "Abby, are you okay?"

CHAPTER ELEVEN

I CLAW AT THE HEAVINESS in my chest and wiggle my left shoulder a little to try to alleviate the sharp twinge in my heart. My vision goes dark for a split second and I blink furiously to hold on.

"Abby, what's wrong?"

Drawing in a large gulp of air, I massage my chest until I can speak. "I'm fine. It's just a spasm."

"Don't downplay it, Abby."

Caleb reaches for my purse, lifting it off the floor where it rests at my feet. Then, he opens the glove compartment to get his emergency bottle of water, and moves right to my purse to retrieve the bottle of Nitrostat.

He hands both the water and the pills to me, but I shake my head adamantly. "I don't need the water," I say, gritting my teeth against the pain.

I place a sublingual tab of Nitrostat under my tongue, grimacing at the heavy peppermint flavor that seeps into my mouth as the pill dissolves. Now, we wait.

Caleb pulls me into his arms and strokes my hair because he knows it calms me. I close my eyes and take slow, deep breaths as I wait for the pill to take effect. About three minutes later, the pain in my chest is gone and my cheeks begin to flush. I push Caleb away so I can fan my face.

"Thank you," I whisper, staring down at the stack of photos, which is now facedown on my lap again.

"Drink this." He hands me the bottle of water and I take a small sip. "How are you feeling?"

"Exhausted."

"Want to go back to the apartment and take a nap?"

I chuckle as I set the bottle of water down on the seat and lightly massage my chest. The pain is gone, but it's relaxing.

"I'm like a senior citizen with my heart medication and frequent napping."

"A senior citizen without the benefit of the early bird special."

I turn to him and my smile vanishes. "What am I going to do if we ever break up? I don't want to live with my parents the rest of my life, with my mom fussing over me while I lie back and wait... wait for the time to come when my only option is a transplant. What kind of life is that?"

"If it's not your mom fussing over you, then it's me. Sunshine, you just have to accept that we love you the way you are, broken heart and all. So I promise never to break up with you, if you promise me you'll take good care of your heart. I might need it one of these days."

I'm burning up, and it must be showing on my cheeks because Caleb grabs a few photos off the stack and uses them to fan my face. I lean back in my seat and close my eyes for a moment while Caleb pampers me. With my eyes closed, my mind wanders to thoughts of heart transplants. I'm pretty close to the bottom of the transplant list right now. I just don't have an urgent need for a new heart. But we all know that the time will come soon when I'm moved up to the top. It could be in ten years, five years, or tomorrow. This heart is a ticking time bomb inside my chest.

The flushing finally passes. I open my eyes and the first thing I see is a wedding picture. Caleb continues to fan my face until I snatch the photos out of his hand.

The pictures he's using to cool me down are obviously from my birth parents' wedding. It's a picture of my father kissing my mother on the forehead as they stand on an altar surrounded by beautiful flowers and glittering lights. They look exactly like they did in the other pictures where they're holding Baby Me. They must have gotten married soon before or after that day. Why did they give me up if they were so in love when I was born?

"I want to meet them."

"You will," Caleb replies as he slides the bottle of water back into his glove compartment.

"No, I want to meet them now… Today. I want you to take me to meet them today. Can you check the memory card and see if there's any contact information on there?"

Caleb slides the memory card into the slot on his phone, then he browses through the contents. There are about forty family videos and one text document. My fingers tingle as he opens up the document and it contains a brief note.

Dear Abigail,

We hope this letter finds you well and that your eighteenth birthday was everything you hoped it would be. This is the second time we're visiting the safe-deposit box since your last birthday, and we will probably do it every month or so for a while. We don't know if you've read any of our letters, but we hope you have.

We know you probably have a lot of questions, and the answers are far more nuanced than a letter can convey. If you'd give us the opportunity, we'd be honored to meet you at any location you choose. We are always here if you wish to talk.

Sincerely,
Chris and Claire Knight

Underneath their names is an address and phone number.

Caleb sits back in the driver's seat, placing his phone down as he gazes at me across the space between us. "Are you sure you don't want to give yourself some time to think about it first?"

I turn in my seat a little so I can face him head-on, then I look him straight in the eye. "I don't know when I'm going to die."

"Come on, Abby. Let's not have that conversation again."

"Listen to me, Caleb. Whether we admit it to ourselves or not, my heart could give out for good at any moment. And there's no guarantee they'll find a donor in time."

"You don't know that. I think there's a very good chance they'll find a donor when the time comes. You have O-negative blood type and you're young and healthy."

"Stop. Just listen to me, please." He heaves a long sigh and nods for me to continue. "The point is that I need to make the most of this opportunity. I need to meet them before it's too late. Will you please take me?"

The muscle in his jaw twitches as he clenches his teeth, then he nods slowly. "You know you don't have to ask. I've been wanting you to do this for ages."

I smile and reach forward to place my hand on his cheek. "You're amazing. You know that?"

He shrugs and grabs my wrist so he can lay a soft kiss on my palm. "You don't have to butter me up, sunshine. You know I'll give you anything you want." He places my hand back in my lap, then he grabs the stack of photos and sticks them in the glove compartment. "Let's go make some 3D memories."

PART TWO:

The Knights

"You may say I'm a dreamer,
but I'm not the only one." - John Lennon

CHAPTER TWELVE

CHRIS

FAITH IS A double-edged sword. A little faith is healthy, even *essential* to get us through difficult times. Too much faith and you'll appear delusional. And you risk falling. The loftier your beliefs, the harder you'll fall when reality knocks you off your cloud.

I've always been a pragmatist. My mother never took me to church as a child. And I sure as hell never found Jesus while on tour for the past two decades. But there's only one secret I've ever kept from Claire, and it's this: For the past eighteen years, I've been going to church and praying for Abigail to come back to me.

No one knows my secret. Not even my best

buddy, Tristan, knows. It may seem like an insignificant thing to keep hidden. And I'm sure Claire would understand why her agnostic husband has been paying regular visits to a small church in West Raleigh for eighteen years. But I haven't kept it a secret because I'm afraid Claire won't understand my need to have a little faith. I've kept it a secret because I'm afraid of how it will affect Claire to know I've been keeping a secret from her for so many years.

I drain the last drops of orange juice from my glass then stick it in the dishwasher. Standing at the kitchen sink, I gaze out the window at the curved driveway in the front of our house in Cary. The sun is shining bright, imbuing everything with a warm glow; the grass, the plants, even Jimi's black Mercedes, they all sparkle in the Carolina sunshine. Today would be a perfect day to go to the beach and get the summer started, if it weren't for that foolish thread of hope tying us to our house in Cary.

For two months, we've been sitting on the edge of our seats, waiting. Every phone call and every knock on the door is met with feverish anticipation. We promised Jimi, Junior, and Ryder we'd leave for the beach house last weekend, but Claire and I both decided we'd wait one more week. It's Saturday. If

Abby doesn't show up by tomorrow night, we'll head out.

I might make a trip to the safe-deposit box tonight. It will be my third visit since Abby's eighteenth birthday two months ago. I keep thinking there will be something in there, a note, a picture, or something telling me she knows about Claire and me but she's not ready. Maybe there'll be a video of her birthday or her high school graduation.

I just want to know that she's okay. It would be even better to know that she doesn't hate us.

We should just gather the kids and head to the beach house tonight. It's been two months. If Abby hasn't come by now, she's not coming at all. I need to accept that I got my hopes up for no reason. Faith is a dangerous thing.

Junior walks into the kitchen with his wireless headphones in his ears.

He nods at me. "'Sup, Dad?"

He heads straight for the door leading to the walk-in pantry and disappears inside. He comes out with a box of cereal. I lean back against the counter and cross my arms over my chest as I watch him. He sets the cereal down on the kitchen island and locks eyes with me. His shoulders slump as he removes the earphones from his ears.

He tucks them into his pocket and heads for the refrigerator. "Where's Mom?"

"She's upstairs. She's not feeling well."

"Migraine?" he asks, bringing the jug of milk to the island.

"No, just tired I think."

He raises his eyebrows as he opens a drawer and grabs a bowl. He knows why she's not feeling well, but no one's talked about Abby for months. As if mentioning her name will break the spell, the illusion that we ever had a chance of having her in our lives.

He opens another drawer to get a spoon, then he settles down at the breakfast bar with his cereal. "So… we're not going to the beach house today?"

"I don't know. I'll see how she's feeling later. Where's your brother? Is he still asleep?"

He shrugs as he shoves a spoonful of cereal into his mouth. He swallows his food then responds. "He went to bed late last night. I heard him playing that new game at two in the morning."

I shake my head at this news. Eleven-year-old Ryder is the quietest of the three kids, and he's very good at testing our limits. But he knows that all it takes to get back in my good graces is to ask me to teach him to play something on the guitar.

Fourteen-year-old Chris Jr. isn't much like me at all. He likes music, but has no interest in learning to play. He plays three different sports, but he doesn't know what career he wants to pursue when he's older. The only thing I think we have in common is our sense of loyalty and our love of fast cars.

Sixteen-year-old Jimi is still my princess. She's always been a daddy's girl and was pretty shy until she started middle school. She began taking acting classes and came out of her shell. I've had lovesick boys knocking on my door for five years now.

I'm about to head upstairs to wake Ryder, when the sound of gravel crunching gets my attention. I turn around to look out the kitchen window and see a red convertible Plymouth Barracuda pulling up behind Jimi's Mercedes. It's a sweet car, but it's the person sitting in the front passenger seat who has my full attention.

I'm frozen as I watch her eyes scanning her surroundings, taking in the house. She hangs her head and the guy in the driver's seat watches her, waiting. Then she looks up again and my heart stops. She sees me in the window.

The seconds tick by in slow motion as I wait for

Abby to move, to smile, to cry, but she looks frozen, too.

"Dad, what are you looking at?" Junior asks.

"Not now," I reply, refusing to divert my attention.

"What is it?" he says, and I can hear his chair scrape across the tile floor followed by the sound of his footsteps.

He's next to me by the sink now and I glance at him to make sure he's seeing what I'm seeing. "Do you see her?" His gaze is pointed in the direction of the red car, but he seems a bit stunned so I ask again. "Junior, do you see her? Please tell me I'm not seeing things."

He nods as a smile curls the corners of his mouth. "Yeah, it's her."

I turn back to the driveway and the car is empty. Junior races toward the front door and I chase after him. It's selfish, I know, but I want to be the one to answer the door for her. I want to be the one to welcome her inside.

"Don't touch that," I say as Junior reaches for the door handle.

"Why?"

"Because I want to do it."

He steps aside and nods. "Hurry up."

My hand reaches forward, but I take my time

pulling the door open. When I finally lay eyes on her, I'm overwhelmed.

Here she is, standing on my doorstep. Looking like an angel. The angel I've been praying for.

Her blonde hair is pulled up in a ponytail and her small hands are clasped in front of her. She's not wearing any makeup. She's naturally beautiful, like her mother.

Claire. I have to go get her. But first, I have to hear my angel's voice.

"Do you want me to get Mom?" Junior whispers and Abby's eyes dart toward him.

She knows that Junior knows who she is. She knows we wouldn't have told Junior about her if we didn't hope he'd meet her someday. And someday is finally here, but I can't speak. My mouth feels wired shut.

"Dad?"

"No," I finally reply, not taking my eyes off Abby. "No, I'll get her."

She looks away from Junior and our eyes meet for a second before she hangs her head. Silent tears roll down her cheeks. Like me, she doesn't know what to say either. We didn't get an instruction booklet on what to say when we met. We're both just overwhelmed by this moment.

"Abigail?" I speak her name softly and she sniffs as she raises her head to meet my gaze. "I've..." I try to swallow the painful lump in my throat, but it doesn't budge. "We've been waiting for you."

She presses her right hand over her heart and begins rubbing her chest.

"Are you okay?" I ask and the guy standing off to the side of her steps closer.

"Abby, what's wrong?" he asks, and that's when I notice he's holding her purse.

It takes a special kind of guy or a special kind of relationship for a guy to hold a girl's purse. Abby and this guy must be in a serious relationship. I try not to think bad things about him, since he obviously seems to care about her well-being. But I guess that fatherly instinct never goes away no matter how much distance or how many years separate you from your little girl.

"I'm fine," she whispers and my heart nearly stops at the sound of her voice.

I've heard her voice on the few videos that Lynette and Brian have shared with us, but they haven't sent us many videos over the past five years. Almost as if they didn't want us to witness her growing from a child into a young adult. But now, hearing her speak right in front of me, not through a speaker, is a dream come true.

"Do you want to come inside?" I offer.

I could probably stand here all day, staring at her and listening to her talk, but I don't want to freak her out. It must feel strange for her to know that we've all been waiting for her.

She shrugs then nods. "Okay."

I step aside so she can enter and it's so difficult not to reach for her. I want to take her in my arms and tell her that I always wanted her. That she never left my mind or my heart.

The guy she's with stands at the threshold, waiting for an invitation. "Come on in," I say and he nods as he steps inside.

"I'm Caleb," he says as I push the door closed.

He holds his hand out to me and I grab it firmly. "I'm Chris and this is also Chris."

Chris Jr. and Caleb nod at each other and I can't help but notice that Junior's grinning. It has to be the Barracuda. He's probably dying to ask this Caleb guy if he can check out his car.

I shoot Junior a look, warning him not to get any ideas, then I turn back to Abby. "Do you mind waiting here for just a moment? I need to go upstairs to get…"

How should I refer to Claire when speaking to Abby? *My wife? Claire? Your mother?* My heart clenches at that last thought. "I have to get my wife. I'll be right back. Please just stay right there."

She nods and I head for the staircase. I glance over my shoulder a few times as I climb the steps, fully expecting her to vanish like an apparition the next time I turn around. But she doesn't. As I head into the upstairs hallway, she's still there. Right where I always imagined she'd be.

Hope: The biggest four-letter word in the English language. It's bigger than despair. Bigger than resentment. Bigger than skepticism. Four letters that, when combined, can hold a broken heart together for eighteen years.

CHAPTER THIRTEEN

Claire

POSITIVE. The test is positive.

I stare at the pregnancy test stick on the marble bathroom counter and shake my head. I can't have another kid at the age of thirty-seven. And I know Chris doesn't want any more kids. He's already planning all the vacations we're going to take once Ryder goes off to college. The honeymoon we never really had after our wedding, when we had to return for Tristan's grandmother's funeral.

Positive.

Are the manufacturers of pregnancy tests trying to tell me that being pregnant at thirty-seven is a positive thing?

No. This is definitely not a positive thing. I thought our days of changing diapers, researching nannies, and struggling through hours of homework help were over.

I grab the pink and white test stick off the counter and hold it up close to make certain that it's a plus sign I'm seeing. It's definitely a plus sign. So that's it. I'm pregnant.

I grab a large wad of toilet paper and wrap it around the test, then I throw it in the waste bin. I don't want Chris to find it. I want to be the one to break the news to him.

"Honey, remember that time twelve years ago when you wanted one more child? Well, better late than never!"

Oh, God. You'd think I'd know better by now. I decided to switch from the IUD birth control to pills. I was getting a lot of cramping and I was afraid of possible scarring. I understood that getting pregnant after having an IUD implant for so many years would be very difficult. We were just waiting for my first menstrual cycle to arrive so I could begin taking the pills. It never came and now here I am.

I grab another large wad of toilet paper so I can push the wrapped test stick to the bottom of the waste bin, but a knock on the bathroom door startles me and I drop the paper into the toilet.

Shit. "Who's there?"

"Babe, it's me. You have to come out here. Now!"

I pull another wad of toilet paper off the roll and hastily stuff it in the waste bin to cover the test stick. As I wash my hands, he knocks again and urges me to hurry up. I dry my hands on a towel then open the bathroom door, ready to yell at Chris for being impatient with me. Then I see his face and I know something is wrong.

"What happened?"

I reach for his face to feel the tears on his cheeks, to know they're real, but he pushes my hand away. I haven't seen Chris cry since he found out I was pregnant with Jimi. His eyes got a bit misty when Joel had a heart attack and Jackie was crying uncontrollably. Just like her son, Jackie rarely cries, so it's always difficult to watch when either of them is overwhelmed by emotion. I almost don't want to know what has Chris this upset.

Chris reaches for my hands, his eyes fixed on them as he pulls my hands together and holds them against his chest. "She's here."

I can't speak or breathe. My chest tightens and I

open my mouth, trying to gasp for air, but I feel as if my throat has closed. As if every emotion I've felt over losing Abby these past eighteen years has suddenly welled up inside me and I'm about to burst.

Chris finally looks up to see my reaction and his eyes widen. "Claire, breathe. Breathe, baby."

I pull my hands out of his grip and cover my face as the first sob spills out, quickly followed by more.

"Claire, we have to hurry up and get down there. I don't want her to leave before you get to see her. Please, babe."

He wraps me in the comfort of his arms and I take a few deep breaths to calm myself. I don't want her to see me like this, but I need to get down there. Finally, I push Chris back and he flashes me a weak smile as I wipe his face clean.

"She's really here?"

He nods and grabs my hands. "She's really here. And she's so damn beautiful... She looks like you and Ryder."

I press my lips together and focus on breathing deeply to keep from breaking down again. "Okay, let's go."

He takes my hand in his and leads me out of the bedroom. I can feel the hope pulsing back and forth between us, surrounding us, giving everything a hazy glow. My heart is thumping so hard, my ears are aching. I grip Chris's hand tighter as he pulls me down the first steps and I hold my breath as we descend. I let it out as soon as I see a blonde ponytail.

I try to focus on breathing, but all that runs through my mind is the one phrase I've imagined saying to Abby for the last eighteen years. The one thing I know I have to say. Junior's face gets serious when he sees me, then Abby and her friend turn around.

My legs suddenly feel too weak to support me. I let go of Chris's hand and reach for the banister to keep from collapsing. Chris reaches the bottom step and turns around. He rushes forward when he sees me teetering on the third step, but I push him away. Everything looks fuzzy as the room pulsates around me, but I'm not going to pass out. I'm just stunned.

Chris holds my elbow as I descend the last few stairs, then I push him away as I take a step toward her. She looks unsure and I'm so afraid of scaring her away. But I have to say what I've been wanting to say.

I take another step toward her, making no attempt to wipe the tears as they slide down my cheeks. I look her in the eye and her lip trembles as the tears begin to fall.

Chris was right. Even with Chris's brown eyes and his nose, she looks like me. It's her blonde hair, the shape of her face, and the uncertainty in her eyes.

"I'm so sorry," I whisper.

I don't know any other way to apologize for the choice I made. A choice she probably knows nothing about. But it's all I want to say. It's the one thing I think she's probably needed to hear from the moment she found out she was adopted.

I wish I knew how she found out. I want to know everything about her and I want her to know everything about us. If I'm being perfectly honest, I want to pretend like the last eighteen years never happened. Like she's been with us all along. I know that can never happen, but I want to believe that this gulf between us is not permanent.

I reach forward slowly until my hand is suspended halfway between us. She stares at it unblinking, her whole body quivering like a leaf. And she's about as thin as one. She's smaller than me and I'm only five-foot-six. I press my lips together as I think of how this is probably due to her heart problems.

The house is so quiet as I wait for her to take my hand or not. Finally, her hand inches forward, slowly, through the distance between us, through the years that have separated us.

I take her hand in mine and she looks up at me, unsure what to do.

I can't shake my daughter's hand. That would be cold, especially when I haven't seen her in more than seventeen years. But am I allowed to think of Abby as my daughter?

I don't know the answer to that question, and I don't care. I pull her into my arms and she lets out a soft puff of air as I squeeze her tight, as if she were holding her breath.

She's so thin, but soft and warm, just the way I remember her. And she smells like a peach blossom. She buries her face in my shoulder, her shoulders bouncing as she sobs silently. I hold on tighter, hoping I can convey how much I've longed for this moment.

"I can't believe you're here," I whisper. "I'm so happy you came… So happy."

Something about these words causes a shift and her sobbing stops. She draws in a long, stuttered breath, then she pulls away from me. The whites of her eyes are so red it makes my heart ache.

She takes a step back, shaking her head as her gaze falls to the floor. "I don't know what I'm doing here."

Chris steps forward so he's at my side. "That's okay. We know this must be very difficult for you." He looks over his shoulder at Junior and snaps his fingers. "Go upstairs and get your brother."

Abby glances up from the floor every few seconds to look at Chris and I think I know what she's thinking.

"Abigail, you probably don't understand any of this right now," I begin, desperation taking hold as I try to think of the right thing to say to make her stay. "But I promise I'll tell you—*we'll* tell you anything you want to know. *Anything.*"

Please just stay.

The young man who came with her steps forward so they're standing next to each other and she immediately turns into him, as if they're magnetized. He wraps his arms around her shoulders and she presses her forehead into his chest as she clutches the front of his shirt. I turn away, wishing I could cover my eyes. I can't watch. It hurts too much to see how much we've hurt her.

Chris comes up behind me and gently grasps my arms to turn me around, so I can face Abby again. To face what we've done. What *I* did.

"Abigail," Chris begins. "We know you—you and

Caleb don't owe us a single second of your time. But we've been waiting for this day for so, so very long. And we're beyond ecstatic that you're here now. Please just give us a chance to explain… everything."

I don't know who Chris is referring to when he says Caleb, but I think it might be the young man holding Abby. He loosens his grip on her and she wipes at her face.

"Are you okay?" he whispers to her. "Do you want to go?"

Please don't go.

Abby sniffs loudly then turns back to us. "I don't know what I expected. I—"

The sound of footsteps descending the stairs gets our attention and all four of us turn toward the staircase. Junior comes bounding down the steps first, wearing a soft smile that fades when he sees the serious looks on all our faces. Following close behind him, I'm not at all surprised to see Ryder coming down in a white T-shirt and blue pajama pants, his blonde hair sticking out in all directions and carrying his guitar in one hand. He always uses that guitar to get himself out of trouble. He must have done something wrong.

"He was still sleeping," Junior says when he reaches the foyer.

"No, I wasn't!" Ryder protests, descending the last few steps. "I was just lying down."

"With your eyes closed and drooling all over yourself?"

Abby and Caleb chuckle and my heart jumps at the sound of her laughter. Junior smiles at her and Caleb, pleased to see he's provided them with some amusement. But Abby's not laughing anymore. Her eyes are fixated on Ryder as he heads straight for Chris to hand him the guitar.

"Can you tune it for me, Dad?"

"Sure. Just hang it up in the studio. I'll do it later." Chris musses up Ryder's hair as he heads for the kitchen with a smile on his face. Chris turns to me, unable to hide his smile. "He was up late playing video games again. That's why he was still asleep. I'll talk to him later."

I shake my head. "Ryder, come back here!"

He groans as he spins around and walks toward me. "What?"

"Don't take that tone with your mom," Chris warns him.

His gaze falls toward the floor. "Sorry."

"It's okay, sweetie," I say, grabbing his guitar and handing it to Chris. Then I grab Ryder by his shoulders to position him in front of me. "Abby—Abigail, this is your other brother, Ryder. I think you met Chris Jr."

She stares at him for a while before she speaks. "It's nice to meet you, Ryder. Do you know who I am?"

Ryder looks up at me with a question in his eyes. He wants to know if it's okay to tell Abby what he knows. I nod and he turns back to her.

He nods vigorously. "I know you. My mom and dad talk about you *all* the time." He starts counting off on his fingers, the way he always does when he's going to say things in a list. "They showed us a bunch of pictures. They showed us videos. They told us to be nice to you. And they said you look like me."

Chris shakes his head and grabs Ryder by the back of the neck. "Stop being a smart-ass and go give your sister a hug."

Abby smiles as he steps forward and wraps one arm around her waist.

"There. Can I go now?" he asks, looking over his shoulder at us with his arm still hooked around his big sister. And now it's so obvious how much they look alike. It's almost frightening.

Abby laughs at Ryder, but Chris shakes his head. "You're treading on thin ice, boy. I know you were up late again."

His shoulders slump. "Sorry."

"You're lucky we have guests here," Chris replies. "Otherwise, you'd be grounded for a week."

I can't help but smile as I watch him being chastised. He never lets go of Abby. Ryder is the most affectionate of the kids, so it doesn't surprise me. But the guarded smile on Abby's face as she looks down at the messy blonde hair on the top of his head fills me with so much joy.

"So I'm not grounded?" Chris shakes his head and Ryder's face beams with relief. He gives Abby a two-armed hug this time then looks up at her. "Thank you!"

Junior is back from the kitchen with a Pop-Tart in his hand. That boy never stops eating and he never gains weight.

"Hey, why don't I get a hug?" he mumbles through a mouthful of food as Ryder races past him into the safety of the kitchen.

"Because you talk with your mouth full," Chris replies.

Junior swallows his food and goes straight to Abby. She pats him on the back as she gives him a friendly hug.

He's smiling as he turns around, then he puts on his best begging face. "Can we go to the beach house now? Please?"

"No, we don't even—" I clear my throat as it begins to thicken. "We don't know how long Abby is going to be here."

My hand flies up to cover my mouth as I realize I called her Abby instead of Abigail. Chris flashes me a look, then he tries to play it off like nothing happened.

"Will you stay for lunch at least?" he asks Abby. "Your sister, Jimi, will be here in about an hour. I know she'd love to meet you."

She lets out a small sigh. "Sister?" She whispers this word, but I can hear the awe in her voice. "Yeah, okay… I guess I can stay for a little while."

I turn to Chris, expecting to see him grinning the way I am, but his smile doesn't reach his eyes. His gaze is locked on Abby and I realize he's the only one who hasn't given her a hug yet. It must be killing him.

I wonder if maybe I should say something, but when I look at Abby, I see that something has passed between them. She's crying again. He steps forward and she goes right into his arms.

CHAPTER FOURTEEN

I SHOULDN'T BE HERE. I'm a bad daughter. My parents would be so hurt if they knew I was standing in this house, seeking comfort in the arms of my biological father. But there's nowhere else I'd rather be.

My tears come so fast, they quickly soak through the patch of T-shirt where my face is buried in his chest. This man whom I never knew, yet I feel like I've known him all my life. At least, I should have known him.

Maybe then I wouldn't have felt so different. So alone. I chose to major in business at NC State because my mom scoffed at my suggestion that I should major in music. And now I see that she didn't discourage me because she thought pursuing a career in music is impractical. She's known who my biological father is all along.

My brother plays the guitar. My father is a famous musician. And he gives the warmest hugs.

I push away gently as this shameful thought crosses my mind. "I'm sorry. I just…" Caleb steps forward and wraps his arm around my shoulder, giving it a light squeeze. "I've been begging my parents to tell me your names and… now I know why they didn't and I don't know if I'm more angry or glad. I'm sorry."

"You don't have to be sorry. Actually, *I* apologize that I didn't introduce us by name. I'm Chris and this is Claire."

"I… I know who you are," I say, suddenly feeling a bit embarrassed.

Now I understand why my mom always tells me to change the song when she passes by my room and hears me listening to a Chris Knight song. I thought she just didn't like his music, though I did find a couple of his old albums in the music library on her laptop. I just assumed she had grown out of that kind of music.

He smiles at me and I get a weird feeling as I recall how I once discussed his hotness with Amy when we were talking about handsome older men. That is so gross. I think Amy even talked about the things she would do with him. *Blech!*

"You know, you can call us whatever you want. You can call us Chris and Claire. You can call us Mr. and Mrs. Knight. You can just say, 'Hey, turkey!' whenever you see me. Whatever makes you comfortable."

Claire smacks his arm then shakes her head. "You can call me Claire or whatever you feel most comfortable with. I... I grew up in the foster care system, so I never really knew how to address the foster parents who took me into their homes. I understand this is probably very weird for you."

I nod and press my lips together to keep from getting emotional. How is it that these people whom I've never met already know me so well?

"Did my parents talk to you about me?"

Chris's face screws up a little as he shakes his head. "No, they didn't communicate with us at all after your first birthday. The only contact we had with them were the photos and videos we exchanged through a safe-deposit box."

"I saw those," I whisper, thinking of the picture I saw of my sister holding a photo of me.

Claire tilts her head. "Do you have the pictures with you? We can go through them with you, if you'd like."

I shake my head. "I don't have them."

I don't feel good about this lie, but there's no way I could sit by and quietly listen as she explains to me all the happy memories that go with each photograph. But there's no nice way to explain that. And, for some odd reason, I really want to be nice to them.

I want to be worthy of the love they have obviously carried for me all these years.

Chris nods toward the kitchen. "Come on. I'll make you guys some lunch."

Caleb finally speaks up. "We just ate a couple of hours ago."

"Actually," I begin. "Do you mind if I go outside to make a phone call?"

"You can make a phone call in here," Claire replies quickly. "I mean, unless you want some privacy. Of course, go ahead. We'll... be right here."

I look up at Caleb then nod toward the front door. He leads the way and we head outside. I know she's not behind me, but I can feel Claire's desire to come after me. Even from across the room and with my back turned. Her desperation is palpable.

As soon as we're outside and Caleb closes the front door behind us, I call Amy. She picks up on the first ring. When Caleb dropped her off at her house, I told her I would call her as soon as I opened the safe-deposit box. That was more than two hours ago and she's probably freaking out.

"What happened?" she shrieks, unable to contain her excitement.

"Amy, I'm here… at my birth parents house."

"*WHAT?*" she yelps.

I hold the phone a couple of inches away from my ear as I continue. "Their contact information was included on a memory card in the box, along with a bunch of pictures. I can't tell you everything or you'll freak out, but I need you to tell my parents that Caleb and I went to his apartment and he's taking me back home tonight. Just tell them I needed some time to cool off."

"Abby, what are you doing? Are you trying to buy some time so you can get a new identity and leave the country with Caleb?"

I laugh. "Just please tell them that. I just need some time to process everything. Okay?"

She's silent for a moment. "Okay. But you'd better tell me everything when you get back. I hate being in the dark."

We say our good-byes and Caleb is smiling at me. "What?"

"You… I don't even know how to say this."

"What? Just say it."

He lets out a soft chuckle and shakes his head. "You've known them for like two seconds and…"

My smile disappears as I anticipate he's going to criticize me for being a bad daughter.

"It's like…" he continues, still trying to find the right words. "Like you've always belonged here."

I slide my phone into my pocket and try to focus on taking deep breaths. "This is all so weird. I never, ever in a million years expected this. I never expected to…" I can't finish this sentence. I can't say that I never expected to be wanted.

Just as this thought crosses my mind, the front door opens and I'm not surprised to see Claire standing at the threshold. "Is everything okay?" she asks as she steps outside.

I nod, but I don't say what I'm thinking. What I'm really thinking is that everything is not okay. It's nowhere close to okay. And I'm totally okay with that.

CHAPTER FIFTEEN

CHRIS

FEAR IS INSIDIOUS. It's a noxious gas that chokes the brain of common sense and motivation. There have been many moments over the past eighteen years when I feared I had become my father.

My father left my mother and me when I was six years old. The few memories he left me with are so hazy I sometimes wonder if he ever existed. At a very young age, I came to an unnatural realization: I didn't miss my father. At first, I thought this was a sign that there was something wrong with me. I tried to fight this part of me that thought it was okay to let go. I even got a tattoo of a pocket watch with the hands stuck at 3:15, the time my father left, to remind me to care. But it didn't work. I never had any desire to meet the father who abandoned me. So the fact that Abby is in my house, to me, is a miracle. It means I have another chance at not repeating my father's mistakes.

I watch with great anticipation as the front door opens and Claire walks in, followed closely by Abby and Caleb. I let out a sigh of relief as they assemble in the foyer and Claire closes the door behind them, wearing the kind of smile I only see her wear when she's with her children.

"Is everything okay?" I ask. "Are you all ready for me to make some lunch?"

Claire comes to me with her hand stretched out before her. She may be smiling, but she usually reaches for me like this when she needs comfort or reassurance. Like me, she's afraid this visit could be cut short at any moment.

I pull her toward me, planting a kiss on her forehead as I slide my arm around the small of her back. "I make a pretty mean grilled cheese," I continue.

"Yeah, Chris took cooking lessons a few years ago when I took a six-week trip to Indonesia. He's a better cook than I am now, not that that's saying much."

A smile pulls at one side of Abby's mouth. "This is

really weird, right? Or is it just me?"

I try not to let the ache in my chest manifest in my facial expression. "It is definitely weird. I can't imagine what it must feel like for you to know that we've always known you existed. You must think... Well, I always hoped that you would understand, to some degree, that a great deal of this situation was out of our control."

I turn to Claire to see her reaction to my words and, as expected, her jaw is clenched and her eyes are beginning to water. No amount of therapy over the past eighteen years could convince Claire that she was not to blame for us losing the battle for an open adoption. No matter how many times I've tried to make her see the truth.

The truth is that the war over Abby began the moment Claire gave her up for adoption. But we lost multiple battles for Abby because of my fame. If I were an electrician like Brian, Abby would have spent the last eighteen years knowing that we always wanted her. Now, we have maybe a few hours to convince her of this.

Abby's smile fades. "I want to know... what happened... I want to know why I wasn't good enough."

I look to Claire again and the tears are flowing freely again. "You were more than good enough. It had nothing to do with you and everything to do with me. I'm the one who gave you up."

"That's not entirely true," I interject, squeezing Claire's shoulder to assure her I'm not going to allow her to throw herself under the bus. "Claire initiated the adoption while I was on tour for my first album. She was afraid I would give up on the tour and my career if she told me the truth. She gave you up so that I could pursue my dreams and so that you wouldn't have to grow up without a father, like we both did."

The way Abby's eyebrows are screwed up, I can see she doesn't know what to believe. And I don't know what to do other than tell her the truth. I have always relied on the truth to cut through the rhetoric and the skepticism. But it seems now that the truth may not be good enough. Claire and I may not be good enough.

Claire steps forward so she's only a couple of feet away from Abby. "Abigail, can I show you something? Before you leave and before you decide this visit was a mistake, there's something I'd like to show you."

Abby hesitates for a moment, glancing up at Caleb, seeking his opinion on Claire's request. Caleb shrugs, and for a moment I fear she's going to tell us she has to leave. Then she nods and I let out a huge sigh.

As expected, Claire slides her cell phone out of the pocket of her jeans and begins swiping her finger across the screen, searching for something. Finally, she stops swiping and she seems transfixed by something on her phone. She takes another step forward and holds it up for Abby to get a better view.

"That's me when I was nineteen and five months pregnant with you. I didn't know my best friend was taking this picture of me. I was lying on the bed in her room, rubbing my belly as I talked to you." She draws in a stuttered breath as she tries to compose herself. "I was promising you that you'd have a better childhood than I did. That you'd never question whether your parents loved you, like I did."

She swipes her finger across the screen again and the photo changes.

"This is a picture you may have already seen," she continues. "This is the first time I held you. You were seven months old and this was the happiest and saddest moment of my life." Claire holds the phone still for a moment before she tucks it into the back pocket of her jeans and steps forward so she's within arm's reach of Abby. "I've wanted you from the moment I found out I was pregnant. There was never, ever a moment where I felt my life was better without you." She reaches forward and Abby allows her to take her hand. "We've been waiting so long to see you, to tell you that we never forgot you. Please stay a while so we can prove it to you."

Abby draws in a deep breath and stares at the floor for a moment before she responds. "How long is a while?"

My heart stutters a bit then pounds wildly. "As long as you want," I reply quickly. "Stay a few hours. Stay the night. Stay—"

"Stay for the summer," Claire interjects and Abby looks up from the floor, her beautiful brown eyes wide with shock.

"The summer?"

I almost want to be angry with Claire for suggesting something so crazy, but the look on Abby's face is telling me that this might not be as crazy an idea as I thought.

"Yes, the summer," Claire continues. "We're headed to our beach house in Wrightsville soon and we'd love for you to spend some time with us there... before you go to college. I mean, if that's what you're planning to do. I'm not trying to be presumptuous."

The corner of Abby's mouth curls up again and she shrugs. "Yeah, I guess you can say I'm going to college."

I tilt my head, trying to figure out what she means by this, but I don't want to pry. "Abby—you don't mind if I call you Abby, do you?"

She shakes her head. "That's what everybody calls me."

I already know this, from our dealings with the Jensens, but I don't mention it to Abby. "Well, Abby, if you don't mind, I'd like to call your parents and see how they feel about you being here before we decide to make plans for the summer."

Claire's head whips around and she glares at me. "She's eighteen years old. I think she's capable of making decisions on her own."

I bite back a retort about how she's still Brian and Lynette's child, and I turn to Abby. "Do your parents know you're here?"

She looks down at the floor again as she replies. "No, they don't know where I am. I had an argument with them this morning, which sort of led me here."

I want to ask what they argued about, but it's none of my business. I just hope it wasn't an argument about coming here to meet us.

"So, is it okay if we call your parents to tell them you're here?"

Claire's face is turned away from me, toward the front door. She's probably cursing me in her head for potentially ruining this visit. But if we want to have any hope of spending time with Abby this summer, her parents have to be brought into the loop. They have cared for her, and her heart, for the past eighteen years. It only makes sense that their approval or disapproval will greatly influence her decision to stay. If she knows we're willing to cooperate with her parents' wishes, she'll know we're willing to do anything to keep her here.

Abby looks up at Caleb and he cocks an eyebrow at her. "Don't ask me. You know I always tell you to be honest with your parents."

Her shoulders slump a bit at Caleb's implication, then she turns to me. "Okay, but…" She bites her lip as she digs for the courage to finish this sentence. "Can you talk to my parents for me? They… my dad said something very hurtful to me this morning and I don't know if I can talk to him right now. Especially after everything I've learned here today."

I clench my jaw tightly shut to keep from asking what Brian said to her. It's best that I don't know. The possibility of an extended stay hangs on my ability to reason with the Jensens. I don't know if I can let Abby stay here knowing she's going against her parents' wishes.

Abby slides her phone out of her pocket and dials the Jensens' phone number. She looks a bit apprehensive as she holds the phone out to me, but I take it without hesitation. I cast a warm smile in her direction as I bring the phone to my ear.

"Abby!" Lynette shrieks into the phone.

"Lynette, this is Chris Knight. Abby is here with us."

"What the hell is going on? Tell her she needs to come home immediately! I cannot believe this! Get Abby on the phone!"

Abby's brow is furrowed as if she were in pain, her gaze pointed at the floor. I could not be more angry with Lynette and Brian Jensen, but I have to remain calm.

"Lynette, Abby is right here, but she's still a little upset over this morning's argument."

"That's none of your business!" Her words are so shrill, my ear starts ringing. "How dare you call me? How dare you talk about her? She's *my* daughter. Not yours!"

I grit my teeth as a surge of emotion overcomes me. I know Abby is not mine to claim. I know it's not my responsibility to protect her from sorrow. But that doesn't mean that I don't feel like she's mine.

"Please listen to me, Lynette. It's not my intention to step on yours or Brian's toes. Abby is... yours. But I think she's old enough to decide if she wants to know us."

Lynette's sniffling makes my stomach writhe. There's some shuffling on the phone, then silence, then...

"Hello?" Brian's voice is deep and lumbering, just the way he looks.

"Brian, this is Chris Knight."

"I know who this is. Where's Abby? Put her on the phone."

I put my hand over the cell-phone speaker and hold it out to Abby. "Your dad wants to speak to you."

Abby shakes her head adamantly. "I don't want to speak to him right now."

I bring the phone to my ear again. "I'm sorry, Brian, but Abby's a little upset right now. We told her she could stay here for a few hours or longer if she needs some time to let things mellow out."

"A few hours or *longer*? What does that mean? Are

you trying to convince her to stay with you? Is that what's going on here?"

"No, that's not at all what's happening. She's the one who came here. We're just offering her a place to cool down."

"To cool down? Did she tell you why she left in a huff this morning? Because Lynette and I refused to let her move in with her boyfriend this summer. Do you still think we're the big, bad, villainous parents now?"

I squint my eyes as I look back and forth between Abby and Caleb. I have no idea how long they've been together. I don't know what kind of guy Caleb is or how he treats her. But I can understand Brian's trepidation. I understand his desire to not let go. I wouldn't want Jimi moving in with her boyfriend after she turns eighteen in a year and a few months. But I highly doubt I could stop Jimi if that was what she wanted to do. And something tells me Abby is just as headstrong as her sister.

"Look, Brian. I don't pretend to know the intricacies of your relationship with Abby or her relationship with Caleb. All I know is that she's upset right now. And she came here to meet us. I think, after all she's been through, that she deserves the chance to decide whether she wants to go home right away."

Brian lets out a puff of laughter. "I knew when she went running, you'd welcome her in."

"Is that a bad thing?"

"I'm not going to waste my time arguing with you about what's good or bad for *my* daughter."

"You're right. I apologize for that comment. But you have to know how important it is for Abby to know that you trust her. You've done... you've obviously done an excellent job raising her. Why not give her the benefit of the doubt that you've raised her well enough to make her own decisions?"

I look up at Abby and she smiles. I don't know if it's because she thinks I made a good point or because she's thankful that I agreed to speak on her behalf. And, truthfully, I don't care. Because that's the moment I realize I'll do anything to keep that smile on her face.

There's nothing but silence on the other end of the line for a moment before Brian finally replies. "If she's too upset to talk right now, tell her to call me when she's not upset. Is Caleb with her?"

"Yeah, he's right here."

"Tell him to make sure she takes her medication. And tell him... to bring her home as soon as she's ready."

My chest puffs up as it floods with warmth. "I'll tell him. Thank you, Brian."

He hangs up without saying good-bye. As amazingly happy and hopeful as I feel right now, I can only imagine that Brian must be feeling the opposite of those emotions. I wish I could feel more sympathy for him, but I'm actually more grateful. I'm grateful that he raised Abby to be the kind of person who would seek us out.

CHAPTER SIXTEEN

Claire

I LEAN AGAINST the counter in the kitchen, the sunlight pouring through the windows, illuminating this moment, burning it into my memory. Abby and Caleb sit at the breakfast bar, watching Chris cook. Ryder is grabbing a heavy cast-iron skillet out of a drawer. Junior is somewhere upstairs, probably on the phone with his girlfriend, Livvy.

"Do you need some help with that skillet?" Chris says as Ryder attempts to lift it onto the cooktop on the island.

"Nope," Ryder grunts. He heaves the pan onto the burner, then Chris high-fives him.

"Nice job, sous chef."

"What's next?" Ryder asks.

Chris launches into his best Julia Child impression and my heart swells when I hear Ryder and Abby laughing together. They even sound alike.

As Chris continues entertaining our guests by pretending to host a cooking show, I slip out of the kitchen and head to the study to call Jimi. Her best friend, Sydney, and Sydney's brother Eric picked her up today to go to a creativity conference where they hope to network with some filmmakers. Eric is studying filmmaking at the Tisch School of the Arts at NYU. He's home for the summer, so Jimi, who plans to pursue an acting career, sees this conference as an opportunity to see how the industry works.

The conference began at nine a.m. and Jimi said she'd be back by noon at the latest. It's ten minutes to noon and I'm getting a bit antsy for her to meet Abby. I dial her number and she picks up on the third ring.

"Hi, Mom."

I can hear a lot of noise and talking in the background. "I hope I'm not interrupting anything at the conference."

"Nope. We were just leaving. Do you need us to pick up anything on the way home?"

"No, thank you. I just need you to come home

quickly."

"Why?"

I'm silent for a moment as I try to maintain my composure, but I'm so overjoyed just thinking the words. It's impossible to say them aloud and not feel overwhelmed.

"She's here, baby… Abby came."

Jimi's silent except for the occasional loud sniff.

"Jimi?"

"I'm here," she whispers, and I can hear her better now that the noise from the conference has faded away.

"Are you okay?"

Another loud sniff, then she clears her throat and responds. "Yeah, I'm fine. I'm just… really happy for you."

"For me? What about you, honey? You finally get to meet your sister."

"Hold on, Mom. I have another call coming in."

She clicks onto the other line before I can respond, then she comes back a minute later. She sounds composed now. No more sniffing or thickness in her throat.

"Mom, that was Jenna. She wants me to help her with her UNC app before we go to the beach house. I have to go."

"Wait a minute. Did you not hear what I just told you? Abby is here and she wants to meet you."

"I can't, Mom. I promised Jenna I would help her with the application before I go to the beach house. Dad told me we're leaving tomorrow. Am I just supposed to let one of my best friends screw up her college application?"

"You said Jenna was getting on your nerves and you were glad she doesn't drive so she can't visit you at the beach house. Those were *your* words!"

"Mom, I don't have time to argue about this. I promise I'll try to finish up quickly."

I shake my head in dismay. "If you miss this opportunity to meet Abby to help Jenna, you will always regret it, Jimi."

"I'll be home as soon as I can. Bye, Mom."

I end the call feeling confused and angry. She seemed overwhelmed with emotion when I told her Abby was here. Then she answered that call and everything changed. It's as if she spoke to someone who convinced her that meeting Abby was a bad idea. My chest hurts at the thought that someone else could have that sort of influence over Jimi.

She's always been a bit of a daddy's girl, but she's

also fiercely independent. She got her driver's license two days after her sixteenth birthday because she was desperate for more freedom. And she completed her college applications all on her own, getting accepted into both NC State and UNC along with a few other universities, like her top pick USC. All she has to do is submit her fall-semester grades to each university this coming January, and she'll have her pick of seven different college campuses.

So, naturally, all of her friends have been asking for her help with their college applications. But I never expected she would choose to put off seeing Abby to help Jenna, a girl who supposedly flirted with Jimi's boyfriend before they broke up three months ago. It makes no sense.

I head back to the kitchen in time to find Chris teaching Abby how to truss a chicken. Ryder is showing Caleb how to work the computer touchscreen on the wall by the breakfast bar. Of course, Ryder shows him how to work the TV function by putting on the Disney Channel.

I sidle up next to Chris and nudge his shoulder with mine. "Jimi's not coming until later."

Both he and Abby turn their heads to gape at me. "Why?" he asks.

"She's helping Jenna with her UNC application and she doesn't want to be a bad friend and ditch her."

Abby's dark-blonde eyebrows scrunch together in confusion. "Is she uncomfortable with me being here?"

"What? No, of course not. She's just become the go-to girl for all her friends who are rushing to get their college applications submitted. It's... unfortunate, but she seems to think we're leaving for the beach house tomorrow. Did you tell her that, honey?"

Chris grabs the salt and pepper off the counter behind us and sets them down in front of Abby. She follows his lead and begins sprinkling the seasoning all over the chicken.

"I may have mentioned that we would be going to the beach house tomorrow, but that was only if... if we had nothing going on. Abby is here now. We're staying here as long as we need to."

Abby holds up her hands and Chris points her to the sink where she can wash the chicken juices and seasoning off her fingers. "You don't have to stay here on my account. Caleb and I have really enjoyed meeting you all, but we don't want to ruin your plans."

"You're not ruining our plans," Chris insists. "You *are* the plans. The reason we were going tomorrow night instead of tonight is because we decided last weekend that we would wait one more week to see if you would show up."

"Aw, that's why, Dad? You lied. You told me it was 'cause of the storm."

Ryder never forgets anything we tell him.

"I didn't lie," Chris says with a grin. "There *was* a storm... in Florida."

Abby smiles as she dries her hands on a kitchen towel, but her smile is barely hiding her disappointment. "Well, maybe Caleb and I should get going so you all can pack and get ready to go to the beach."

"No, you don't have to go," I reply hastily. "In fact, why don't you stay the night and you can go with us to the beach house for a few days?"

Chris narrows his eyes at me then turns back to Abby. "We don't want you to feel pressured or obligated to stay. But, of course, you are welcome to stay as long as you want."

"You should come with us to the beach house!" Ryder's eyes are wide with excitement. "The beach is right there and last year there was a shark in the water and everyone was taking pictures of it with their phones and this one lady screamed and everyone thought she was bit, but she wasn't."

"I... I don't know. I mean, I don't want to impose."

"Don't be silly. You're not imposing," I insist.

"But I don't think I'd feel comfortable without Caleb."

"He can come," I reply.

"Yeah!" Ryder agrees.

"Why are you so happy?" Junior says, walking into the kitchen with his nose buried in a text conversation.

"Abby and Caleb are coming with us to the beach house!" Ryder replies.

"Settle down, Ry. Nothing is decided yet," Chris says, taking the remote away from him so he can turn off the TV.

Ryder crosses his arms and glares at Chris, but Chris glares right back at him. After a moment, Ryder smiles. "Thanks for turning the TV off, Dad. It was rotting my brain."

Chris shakes his head. "Go upstairs and take a shower. Now."

"You guys are coming to the beach house? Sweet!" Junior says, taking a seat on the stool next to Caleb at the breakfast bar. "Maybe you can give me a driving lesson in your car?"

Caleb chuckles. "You got a permit?"

Junior waves off the question. "A mere technicality."

Abby stands across the breakfast bar from Caleb, their eyes locked, and I can feel them silently communicating, gauging the other's reaction. He nods slightly and she nods back.

"Well, I guess as long as I have my meds and my parents know where I am, it should be okay for a few days," Abby begins, turning away from Caleb to face Chris and me. "I mean, neither of us have been to the beach in a long time."

"Do you like the beach?" I ask.

She smiles at this simple question that still seems to say so much about how desperate I am to know her. "Yeah, I love it, but because of my heart condition, it's not good for me to engage in a lot of physical activity. My parents used to take me swimming at the aquatic center all the time, but they thought the waves and currents of the ocean were too unpredictable to be safe."

I nod my head, though I really just want to take her in my arms and tell her how sorry I am that we didn't give her a better heart. "Well, you'll be safe with us. We won't let you out of our sight."

"Neither will I."

Abby turns to Caleb after he says this and the expression on her face is full of adoration. Abby and Caleb are not just boyfriend and girlfriend. They're in love. He takes care of her, the way Chris has always taken care of me.

Six hours later, we dine on Chris's famous slow-roasted chicken. All the men and boys retire to the living room to watch a sci-fi action flick while I lead Abby upstairs to show her the guest room where she will be sleeping tonight. I had planned to have Jimi show Abby around, to give them a chance to chat, but Jimi still hasn't come home.

We arrive at the guest room, where I stop outside and point at the double doors at the end of the hallway. "That's our bedroom down there. If you should wake up in the middle of the night and need something, glass of water, extra blanket, anything, just go ahead and knock. We're both light sleepers."

I show her around the guest room and the attached guest bath, then I realize she has no clothes to change into for bed. I take her to Jimi's room to get some pajamas for her to borrow.

"It's fine. I can sleep in this," she insists.

"Oh, don't be silly. Jimi's friends are always borrowing her clothes. She won't mind."

"I won't mind what?"

We both whip our heads around and find Jimi standing at the doorway with her friend Sydney. Jimi's long, light-brown hair falls in soft waves over her shoulders and her blue eyes are focused on me awaiting my response.

"Jimi, come over here and meet your sister."

Jimi waits a few seconds before she turns her attention away from me and onto Abby. She walks slowly, almost reluctantly, toward us until she's a few feet away. Crossing her arms over her chest, she waits for me or Abby to say something.

Abby looks at her for a couple of seconds then turns to me. "Did I do something wrong?"

"Of course not." I glare at Jimi, letting her know that I am not impressed with her attitude.

"Of course you didn't do anything wrong," Jimi says in a sugary voice, the voice she uses when she's being sarcastic.

I hope Abby doesn't notice it, but the confused look on her face tells me she's definitely sensed the chill in Jimi's tone. I place my hand on Abby's back and lead her toward the door.

"I expected better from you," I say to Jimi as we pass her. "Much better. And you, Sydney. It's time for you to go home."

Sydney flashes Jimi a tight smile as she heads for the door. "I guess I'll see you when I see you."

"Yeah, like, never," Jimi mutters as she heads for her closet to put away her shoes.

I close her door and say good-bye to Sydney as she descends the stairs. Abby looks a bit stunned as she heads toward the staircase. I grab her hand and she stops in the middle of the corridor, but she doesn't turn around to look at me.

"I'm sorry for the way she behaved. I didn't expect that from her at all. When I called her on the phone earlier to tell her you were here, she seemed genuinely happy. Abby, please look at me."

She's still for a moment, then she turns around slowly. But she doesn't look at me, she looks at the pictures hanging on the wall. The upstairs hallway of both the beach house and this house are lined with pictures of the kids, including Abby. We took our pictures of Abby down when Jimi was a baby because it was too painful for me to deal with. But after Ryder was born, we put them back up, when we realized how important it was that they know Abby and how much she means to us.

"They've all grown up with me," she whispers, then she turns to me. "I guess it only makes sense that they feel differently, more comfortable, than I do."

I nod in agreement as I realize she's making an excuse for Jimi's behavior. She's trying to imply that Jimi is only treating her the way they would treat each other if they'd grown up together. Just the way Chris makes excuses for me and my choice to give Abby up for adoption. She may look like Ryder and me, but Abby is truly her father's daughter.

CHAPTER SEVENTEEN

THE PHONE CALL TO my mom did not go well. I knew she wouldn't like the idea of me staying the night here, but I'm not ready to go home yet. From the moment I stepped out of Caleb's car this morning until now, I've had one thought simmering in my mind: If my birth parents are so successful and they really seem to care about me and want me in their lives, why would my parents want to keep me from meeting them?

The only answer I keep coming up with is that they were afraid I would prefer my birth parents to the mom and dad who raised me. That's absurd. Along with Caleb, my mom and dad are the ship I've floated on for eighteen years. They've saved my life countless times. They've suffered with me through every illness, every surgery, every sleepless night. They were there cheering me on at every game, every award ceremony, every triumph. My adoptive parents didn't just choose me; they fought for me.

I don't want to hurt them, but they shouldn't have let their fear affect their decisions. They should have known that I will never stop loving them. That I will never choose my birth parents over them.

They shouldn't have hurt me to keep themselves from getting hurt.

Caleb glances over his shoulder to where the door to this guest room stands wide open. He turns back to me and sighs, and I worry that he's going to tell me that staying the night here is a bad idea. It does seem impulsive, but it also feels like my only chance to understand the other half of me.

For eighteen years, I've known one part of me. The part that was raised by Brian and Lynette Jensen. But now, seeing how similar I am to my biological parents, I understand why there was a huge part of me that always felt disconnected. As if I would never be able to be myself around my parents. That doing the things that made me happy was an affront to them. Like pursuing music. I'm a real-life experiment in nature versus nurture. And I don't know which part of me is larger, but I think I owe it to myself to find out before I go to NC State to major in *business*.

"Go ahead. Tell me I'm making a mistake."

Caleb smiles and shakes his head. "Not at all what I was thinking. I was actually just thinking that I hope they have less bedrooms in the beach house so we're forced to sleep in the same room."

I roll my eyes. "Go to your room. I have to try to get some sleep."

"Did you take your Lasix?"

"I took all my meds. Now go, before they think we're doing something in here."

He chuckles as he leans in to kiss my forehead. "Goodnight, sunshine."

WAKING UP IN SOMEONE else's bed two nights in a row is not something I'm used to. So when I open my eyes and realize that, for the second time in a row, I slept peacefully through the night, it feels meaningful. Why should I feel comfortable sleeping in a home with a bunch of people who are essentially strangers?

The sunlight spilling through the window makes all

the white furnishings and linens appear as if they're glowing from within. Like I woke up in heaven. I throw off the covers and sit up slowly so I don't get lightheaded. I don't even notice I'm doing it anymore, but it took me about three years to get used to getting out of bed slowly.

I've always been an early riser, partially because my heart condition makes me tired, so I rarely stay up late unless I'm with Caleb or my friends. But I also like waking up early to see the sunrise. Here in North Carolina, we don't get dazzling sunsets like they do on the West Coast. But we have some of the most gorgeous sunrises. A symphony of colors: Magenta transitions into a vibrant coral then becomes a soft tangerine bridge, leading to a finale in various shades of gold.

That's it. That's why I feel so comfortable here. Because the Knight family understands how music makes everything more beautiful.

The Knight family. My stomach vaults at these three words and I begin to have delusional thoughts of Chris Knight using his clout to get me a contract with his label. It's stupid and dangerous to think things like that. That kind of craziness could cloud my judgment. Make me do things I wouldn't normally do. Like going to stay at a beach house a hundred miles away from my parents.

But Chris and Claire are my parents, too.

Oh, God. This is hopeless. I feel like Chris's famous roast chicken, like I'm being carved into pieces: one piece for my mom and dad, one for the Knights, one for Caleb and my friends. How about me? Which piece of me do *I* get to keep?

The piece that has to go to college for four years to study a subject I have little interest in.

On this depressing note, I rise from the bed determined to fill this summer with new experiences. I want to tread into the salty ocean. I want to build a sandcastle with Ryder. I want to blast the music in the 'Cuda while taking Junior for a joyride.

I haven't decided yet what I want to do with Jimi. Something tells me she feels a bit threatened by my presence, but I can't see why. She has everything I've never had. She probably has tons of friends. She's younger than me but she's taller, so she obviously doesn't have a heart condition. And, by the looks of it, she has every luxury she could possibly want. I guess her behavior says less about the things she has and more about the things she's afraid of losing.

A knock at the door startles me. "Who is it?" I call

out, scrambling toward the desk in the corner where the jeans and T-shirt I was wearing yesterday are neatly folded.

"It's me."

I sigh with relief at the sound of Caleb's voice. "Come in."

He pushes the door wide open and smiles when he sees me. "Good morning."

"Close the door. I have to change."

He looks confused. "With me in here?"

"No, of course not. Go wait outside."

He cocks an eyebrow as his gaze slides from my face and down the length of my body. "I'll be right outside," he says with a sly grin, "using my X-ray vision."

"Get out of here."

Once I've changed out of the pajamas I borrowed from Claire, I come out of the bedroom and find Caleb having a conversation with Junior about cars. Junior nods at me, his way of saying good morning, I guess.

"Good morning. Is everyone awake?"

"Yeah, except Ryder. As usual." He looks to Caleb, his eyes wide. "Hey, we should go cover him in shaving cream and post a video of it on Facebook."

Caleb pats his arm. "You're on your own there, man."

Junior's shoulders slump, but he follows closely behind us as we head downstairs. Jimi, Claire, and Chris are in the kitchen cooking what smells like bacon and waffles. Chris is ladling batter into a waffle iron while Jimi fries the bacon in an iron skillet. Claire is unloading the clean dishes from the dishwasher. Junior heads straight for the breakfast bar, not bothering to offer his help as he grabs the remote and turns on the TV/computer.

"Is there anything we can help with?" I say.

Chris turns away from the waffle iron. "Hey, there. Good morning."

"Good morning, Abby," Claire says, smiling at me as she stacks up some plates in a cupboard.

Chris nudges Jimi's arm and I can hear her sigh before she turns her head to flash me a stiff smile. "Good morning."

"Sweetheart, we don't need any help," Claire says, grabbing the utensil tray out of the dishwasher. "You two just sit down and relax. Breakfast is almost ready. Chris's famous waffles."

"That's lame, Mom. Not everything Dad makes is famous," Junior says as he flips through the TV channels.

"He made you, didn't he?" she replies.

Junior scrunches up his face in disgust. "Gross. Can we please save the sex talk for after breakfast?"

Jimi laughs at this and I cover my mouth to hide my smile, but Caleb lets out a brief guffaw. Claire and Chris glare at Junior, unimpressed.

"You're lucky your brother isn't here, or you'd be grounded," Claire says. "Now set the table."

Junior rolls his eyes then heads into the kitchen to grab some plates, glasses, and silverware. I offer to help him, but he refuses, nodding toward his parents to imply they'd be upset if he enlisted my help.

Once the table is set, Junior sits on the other side of Caleb while Claire sits on my other side. Chris sits next to Claire and Jimi sits between him and Junior.

"How about Ryder?" I ask.

"He'll eat when he wakes up. I try not to wake the kids up too early in the summer."

"You didn't mind waking me up this morning," Jimi says, cutting a piece of waffle and stabbing it with her fork.

"That's because you're grounded, and part of being grounded is losing privileges, like waking up late," Claire replies.

Jimi doesn't respond, so Chris leans over and whispers something in her ear. Her nostrils flare as she purses her lips together, trying to maintain her composure. But tears begin to well up in her eyes and she throws down her fork on the plate and rises from the table, storming out of the breakfast nook without another word.

"What did you say to her?" Claire asks when Jimi is gone.

Chris continues to cut his waffle, unimpressed with Jimi's emotional exit. "I told her that I locked her cell phone in the safe. She's not bringing it to the beach house."

Caleb and I glance at each other, unsure what to say. I don't know if I should acknowledge that I'm the reason Jimi is in a bad mood. Maybe I should just offer to leave. I open my mouth to speak, but Chris puts up his hand.

"Don't let her get to you. This has nothing to do with you being here."

"I'm not sure that's true," I reply. "I really don't want to ruin her summer."

Claire stares at the plate of waffles in the center of the table and Chris grabs her hand before he looks me in the eye. "I'll admit that I've spoiled Jimi. After losing you, it was hard not to channel all the love we felt for you into her. We doted on her and treated her like a princess. But we also raised her to be loving and helpful. She knows that we've been looking forward to meeting you for a very long time. She may be sixteen, but she's a bright girl. She knows this behavior is not welcoming. So she'll just have to deal with the consequences of her actions until she decides she's ready to approach this situation from a place of maturity."

I nod when he's done speaking. For some reason, I feel a bit chastised, like I'm not allowed to stick up for Jimi. Then I realize, this is what it feels like to have siblings. You fight and your parents try to keep the peace. But, inevitably, someone ends up in trouble. Then a bit of time passes and everyone loves each other again.

I don't like being a source of anguish for Jimi, but maybe this tension will change us for the better.

"You want to ride with us to the beach house?" Caleb asks Junior, and I'm grateful to put an end to the heavy silence.

"Really? Can I drive?"

Chris and Caleb laugh. "No, but I'll put the top down and you can sit in the back."

"I'll take that."

I glance at Claire and she's smiling at Junior. Then she reaches across the table and squeezes Chris's hand. "Go talk to her."

Chris nods and turns to Caleb as he stands from the table. "Are you sure you don't mind taking him with you?"

"Not at all. I like his style," Caleb replies and Junior grins.

Chris looks a little leery of Caleb's friendliness, as if he suspects Caleb of trying to get on his good side. I smile as I realize I have *two* fathers who want to protect me from Caleb. How lucky am I?

CHAPTER EIGHTEEN

"MAKE IT QUICK," Claire says, grabbing my wallet off the dresser and handing it to me. "I want to make it to the beach house before eight. And... I have a surprise for you."

"A surprise?" I say, tucking my wallet into the back pocket of my jeans. "Does it involve nudity?" I grab her hips and pull her toward me so her breasts are pressed against my chest.

She lets out a nervous giggle as I brush my lips over the length of her slender neck. "Maybe. Just hurry up, okay?"

I take her face in my hands and look her in the eye. "In that case, I'll be back in a flash. Do I need to pick up anything on the way home? Massage oil? Whipped cream? Batteries?"

She shakes her head and pushes me away. "Just go have your drink and come back soon."

I slap her ass as I walk out of the bedroom and she yelps. "See you later, babe."

I rush out of the house and slide into the driver's seat of my Jaguar. One of my many regrets I have as a father is that I taught my children to appreciate the feeling of being behind the wheel of a fast car. I used to set Jimi and Junior in my lap when they were much smaller and let them steer while I drove around empty parking lots. I regret it because now they refuse to drive the safer self-driving cars. They want to grab that steering wheel and command the road.

Normally, I ride my motorcycle everywhere during the summer, but there's a chance of rain today, so I'll stick to the Jaguar. Last thing I need is to have my bike slide over a slick road and into a busy intersection just hours before I'm supposed to go to the beach house to spend the summer with my firstborn.

My Abby.

I park the Jaguar next to Tristan's new Tesla and head straight into the pub. He's sitting on the second to last stool at the end of the bar, as usual, and nursing a draft beer while laughing about something with Link. Link bought the bar about ten years ago when the previous owner retired. So, naturally, Tristan Pollock has spent the last ten years getting drunk on Link's dime.

His shoulder-length light-brown hair flies all over the place as he points his finger in Link's face and laughs. "Ha! I knew it was you at that fucking show. You don't have to pretend with me, bitch."

Link shakes his bald head. "I don't know why you're talking shit. You were at the same fucking show."

"Yeah, but I was there with my daughter. You were there with your girlfriend. That's some sick shit."

I take a seat on the last stool. "What show are you talking about?"

"Defy This show at Walnut Creek last Sunday."

I shake my head. "I'm glad Jimi is past that stage." Link slides a draft beer to me and I down a few big gulps. "So what happened with Xander? Did you talk to Estelle?"

Estelle Greenway is Xander's sister. Xander was my manager for twelve years until we parted ways over a contract dispute. We've stayed in touch for the past eight years, though we hadn't spoken to each other in about five months when Estelle contacted me last week. Xander has been in the hospital for three weeks with persistent pneumonia and, despite the doctor's best efforts, his condition continues to decline. I visited him in the hospital on Friday afternoon, but he was in a medically induced coma and on a ventilator. Tristan was supposed to visit him yesterday to see how he was doing.

Tristan shakes his head. "It's not good, man. Estelle said they're taking him off the ventilator on Wednesday if he doesn't improve."

I grit my teeth against the anger. "It's a fucking lung infection. You'd think they could just give him some fucking antibiotics. This is no way for him to go."

Tristan shrugs. "I don't know. Estelle looked pretty relieved about it. She's been watching him suffer for weeks. That's no way for him to *live*."

I don't want to get into an argument about life and death with Tristan, so I change the subject. "I'm going to the beach house tonight."

Tristan downs the rest of his beer and grabs the new one Link just set down for him thirty seconds ago. "I know. You told me that on the phone."

"Yeah, but I didn't tell you who's coming with

me."

Tristan squints his eyes as he stares at the pint glass in front of him. "Wait a minute. Are you saying…?"

I nod and let out a sigh. "She came to our house yesterday."

Link sets another beer down in front of a customer a few seats away then rushes back to join the conversation. "Who came to your house?"

"Look at this nosy hen," Tristan remarks.

"Abigail, my first daughter. The one… we gave up for adoption eighteen years ago."

I've told Link about Abby before, but it was at least a decade ago. I wouldn't expect him to remember. And as much as it pains me to say that *we* gave her up for adoption, I've always stood behind Claire's decision. Because I know her decision to give Abby up was made completely out of love for me. I can't show my gratitude to her by blaming her every chance I get.

"So what does that mean?" Tristan asks. "She's going to the beach house with you all this summer? Do you think that's a good idea?"

"I don't know, but there's no way I can convince Claire that it's not. So I'm going along with it for now. And, I gotta admit, it feels really fucking good to have her with us."

"Is she there right now?"

"Nah, she went home to pack some things. She took Junior with her. They're driving to the beach house with her boyfriend tonight."

"Sounds like a perfect family reunion. Now I know why you called this emergency meeting."

I slide the beer away and turn to Tristan. "Listen, I know Senia's busy with Izzy's dance stuff, but can you make sure she checks up on Claire? I know she's going to need to talk to Senia over the next week or so. However long Abby decides to stay."

Tristan's eyebrows shoot up and he laughs. "Are you fucking kidding me? When I tell Senia about Abby being at the beach house, she'll probably pack up the whole fucking family and drive down there herself."

I let out a soft chuckle. "I guess so. Then, maybe don't tell her right away."

He turns to me with one eyebrow cocked. "Now you've really gotta be kidding me. You know I can't keep shit from her."

"All right, fine. Just don't tell her I want her to check up on Claire."

We sit for a few minutes in silence, just sipping our beers, then Tristan clears his throat, like he's getting ready to say something very serious. "So what do you want to do about Xander?"

"What do you mean?"

"Are you gonna come back for the funeral?"

I press my lips together as I contemplate this question. "Don't talk about him like that. He's not dead yet." I slide off the barstool and nod at Link. "Later, man."

THE HOUSE IS QUIET as I climb the steps to the second floor. My home is rarely quiet, so it always raises the hairs on my neck when I walk through the door and I'm greeted with silence. I enter the bedroom and see the door to the master bathroom is closed. I approach slowly, listening for the sound of running water, but I hear nothing. I raise my fist to knock on the door, but it opens on its own.

Claire screams when she sees me. "Shit! You scared me. I didn't know you'd be back so soon."

"Why are you naked? Are you taking a shower?"

She looks over my shoulder at the bedroom door. "Close the door!"

I smile as I turn around and head over to pull it

closed. Then I lock the door, for good measure. When I turn around, she's at the dresser, sifting through her panty drawer. I come up behind her and nuzzle my face in her neck so I can taste her skin.

"Where are the kids?" I murmur into her ear.

"Jimi took Ryder to get a new bodyboard. They just left."

"Good."

"Chris?" she whispers, her back arched as I slide my hand between her legs. "Remember that surprise I told you about?"

My finger slides between her flesh and she lets out a soft squeak when I find her clit. I pull her backward, away from the dresser, then I gently lay her belly-down on the bed. Sliding my left hand down the back of her left thigh, I pull it sideways to spread her legs.

"You said the surprise might involve you being naked, so I'll just come right out and say that I *really* like this surprise." My hand glides between us to undo my pants and she laughs. "What's so funny?"

She tries to turn around, but she can't with me lying on top of her. "Get up. I need to turn around."

"Okay, fine. No doggy style today."

I stand up so she can flip onto her back, but the minute I see her ample breasts trembling with movement, the sinful curve of her hips, and the light patch of hair on her mound, I can't resist. I get right back on top of her and she laughs as she pushes me back.

"I'm serious, Chris. I have to talk to you."

I roll my eyes as I stand up again and offer her my hand to help her up. "What could be more important than having sex right now? All the kids are gone. *All* of them."

Her face suddenly gets very serious and I could kick myself as I remember Abby is now included in that statement.

"Sorry. I didn't mean it the way it sounded."

She waves off my apology and reaches for my face. "I know you didn't mean it that way. You're the most amazing father and person I've ever known. Which is why I'm kind of glad that I get to tell you this without anyone else around. You deserve that."

"You're kind of worrying me right now, Claire. What's going on?"

She gazes into my eyes, not blinking as she draws in a large breath and lets it out slowly. "I'm pregnant."

My body suddenly feels very heavy. I blink a few times then stare at her, expecting her to tell me this is a joke, but the punchline never comes.

"You're serious?"

She nods, her eyebrows screwed up with worry. "Are you angry?"

"What? No. Of course not. I'm just… stunned. I mean, I haven't heard those words come out of your mouth in twelve years. I think I'm a little rusty on how to react."

"Well, jumping up and clicking your heels together is always an option."

I laugh as I take her face in my hands. "I'm sorry. You definitely caught me off guard, but I know we can do this. We've done it before. It's just that I had so many plans for us, but it's no big deal. We've been all over the world for shows. I'm sure those places won't be that much better without a show to play." I kiss her slowly, sucking gently on her top lip until I get a soft whimper out of her. "Ooh, now we can have pregnant sex again."

"Are you really okay with this? This is going to be number five. And this body isn't getting any younger or prettier."

"This body could not be more beautiful. Lie down."

She manages a tiny smile as she lies back on the bed. I lie next to her and place my hand on her belly.

"This body has carried and given birth to our four children." I lean down and kiss the soft flesh below her navel. "This body gets up at the crack of dawn every day to make my life easier." I plant another kiss just below her breastbone. "This body yields to my every desire." I take her nipple into my mouth and she sucks in a sharp breath as I suck on her flesh. My fingertips skate over her waist and hips, tripping over the soft curves of her flesh, until I reach her succulent ass. Then I bring my hand forward and slide it between her legs. "This body is mine." I bury my finger inside her and she gasps. "Say it."

She moans as I dig deeper inside her. "My body is yours."

I spread her legs so I can position myself between them. Then, I lie down, keeping pressure inside of her with my right hand as I use my other hand to spread her sweet flesh. I French-kiss her clit, savoring the slight tang of her skin. This is Claire's favorite way to orgasm, when I kiss her clit as if it were her mouth, which means it's my favorite thing to do to her. Her panting quickly becomes louder, so I ease off a bit. Pulling my finger out of her, I switch to lightly kissing her swollen lips and tracing my tongue up and down her slit.

She whimpers softly, her flesh engorged and hips rocking slightly back and forth as her need increases. "Please, make me come."

I slide two fingers inside her and lightly run my tongue over her hard nub.

"Oh, Chris," she breathes as I gently suck on her clit. "Oh, God, Chris. Don't stop."

She grabs the comforter and pulls it over her mouth to muffle her screams. Her hips buck wildly, so I slow down. Lightly sucking on the flesh around her clit. Teasing her until I can see her juices running over my hand.

I turn my fingers around and press down on the rear wall of her vagina and once again take her clit into my mouth. She cries out, spasming with pleasure as I devour her while I thrust my fingers down firmly and repeatedly, simulating the sensation that she's being fucked hard from behind. Another one of her favorite positions.

"Oh, fuck!" she yelps, though her cries are muffled by the blanket. "Oh, Chris! I'm coming!"

I smile as I gently press my forearm down on her abdomen to hold her steady. I close my lips around her clit again and flick my tongue quickly as I suck. She's not bucking anymore, but her thighs are convulsing as she reaches for my hair.

"Oh, my God!"

I can feel her wetness all over my chin. She tries to yank me up by my hair, but I push her hands away. I'm going for orgasm number two.

CHAPTER NINETEEN

Claire

THE DRIVE TO THE BEACH house is filled with questions from Ryder about what we're going to do when we get there. "Can we go swimming tonight?… Is Abby there already?… That's not fair I didn't get to go with Junior. Can I ride in Caleb's car when they get there?… Are we going to the music festival again?… Is Abby sleeping in my room? She can sleep in my room. I don't mind."

"Abby will be sharing a room with Jimi," I reply to Ryder.

He slumps in his seat and pouts the rest of the way there. I hope Jimi reacts better than Ryder when I give her this same news.

Chris pulls into the driveway of the beach house and I let out a sigh of relief. The gray siding and white trim were Chris's idea, which I was opposed to at first. But, as usual, he was right. The house has a very elegant Cape Cod feel with a few homey touches, like the decorative cornices and the large wraparound porch. I love the big house in Cary, but the beach house feels more like home to me. Maybe that's because Wrightsville was my home when Chris and I got back together more than seventeen years ago.

Jimi pulls her Mercedes into the driveway about three minutes after Chris. He takes all the luggage up to the bedrooms with Ryder's help while I grab some linens from a closet and get them into the washing machine. I come out of the upstairs laundry room and head straight for Jimi's bedroom.

"Why do I have to share my room?" Jimi shrieks. "My room only has one bed! Ryder has bunk beds!"

"We have the rollaway bed in the garage from when Grandma and Grandpa stayed over. She can sleep on that," I reply. "We'll just have to move stuff around to make room."

"Why can't Ryder and Junior share a room? Then she can stay in Ryder's room with her boyfriend."

"She's not sharing a room with her boyfriend,"

Chris replies as he and Ryder enter with the rollaway bed. "She's sharing a room with you, so get over it."

"This is so unfair. How can you be so naive? They've probably already had sex. You guys were having sex at their age."

"Ew!" Ryder shouts, covering his ears with his hands.

"Enough!" Chris barks at her. "This isn't up for negotiation. It's a done deal. Now, let it rest."

Jimi shakes her head, tears glistening in the corners of her eyes. I definitely need to have a chat with Jimi before Abby arrives. I just hope I can clear some of this tension. I always expected there would be a little awkwardness between Abby and the kids when she came back to us. But I never expected it would last more than a couple of hours. I don't know how long this is going to last. All I know is that if it lasts much longer, it will break my heart, just as it was finally beginning to mend.

"Honey, can you run to the store and get a few extra pillows? I forgot we had to throw some out last time we were here when Ryder got sick."

"Oh, yeah. I forgot about that. Yeah, I'll run out and get some in a little while." Chris tests out the bed to make sure it's locked in position, then he looks around the room. "I'll get Junior to help me move this furniture around later."

"Caleb can help you," Jimi says.

Chris flashes her a look, then he seems to decide not to address this comment. "I'll take Ryder with me to the store. You need anything else?"

"Yeah, get some eggs and stuff so I can make breakfast tomorrow."

"Will do, babe."

He plants a quick kiss on my temple then squeezes his way through the tight space between the two beds. I sit on the bed next to Jimi and wait until I hear Chris and Ryder are gone before I speak.

"I know this is difficult for you."

"I don't want to talk about this, Mom."

She opens the top drawer of her nightstand and pulls out a set of wireless headphones. I grab the headphones before she can put them on.

"Don't do that. I'm trying to have a conversation with you. Talk to me, Jimi. I want to hear your side of this. I want to make this easier for you."

She lets out a short burst of laughter, and I fully expect her to make a caustic comment about how much I don't care. Then her eyes begin to water and she pulls her legs up onto the bed so she can hug her knees to her chest and hide her face.

"Oh, honey," I murmur, brushing her long light-brown hair back so it's not covering her eyes. "I hate to see you this way. Please talk to me."

"I'm not crying because of Abby or my stupid phone. I'm just upset. I... I got in a fight with Sydney and now this whole summer is going to suck. I just hate everything right now."

Jimi has always had a problem talking about her feelings. Now she's making up some excuse about a fight with Sydney to avoid the topic. I scoot a bit closer and wrap my arms around her shoulders. Then I lean my forehead against hers and she lets out a soft sob. Straightening out her legs on the bed, she lays her head on my shoulder as I pull her closer.

"I'm sorry," she blubbers into my neck. "I don't want to ruin this for you."

I squeeze her tighter. "Don't apologize. You're not ruining anything."

"Yes, I am. But I can't help it."

I stroke her hair and kiss the top of her head. "Jimi, I don't want you to set your feelings aside. You have a right to feel what you're feeling."

"No, I don't. This is supposed to be a happy time... for you."

I release my hold on her and lean back so I can look her in the eye. "You have a right to feel scared. And I love that you don't want to share us. I don't want to share you with anyone else either. Hint-hint, Jared."

She lets out a congested chuckle at my mention of the cute boy she's been exchanging text messages with since the last day of school a week and a half ago.

"But listen to me, Jimi. Just because I don't want to share you doesn't mean that you don't need me to. You need the love of your friends as much as you need my love. And I need to have Abby here as much as I need you. I love you both, baby. And I know it's probably difficult for you to understand how I can love her so much after all these years. I wish I could explain it, but I can't. It's just love. It doesn't make sense. And it doesn't mean I love *you* any less. It doesn't mean you're not still your father's princess."

She sniffs loudly and nods as she stands from the bed. "I'm going to take a shower."

I stand up after her and turn around when I get to the door. "I love you."

"Love you, too."

I close her bedroom door behind me to give her some privacy, then I pull my phone out of my pocket and dial Senia's number. I called her this morning after Chris left to meet Tristan, and I told her everything. She wanted to come to my house right then and there, but I told her the kids were all gone already. Senia is still the only friend who will drop everything to be there for me when I need her. As she still likes to say, she's my sister from another mister.

"What happened?"

"What kind of way is that to answer the phone?" I say, descending the last few steps and heading straight for the kitchen.

"Sorry, I'm just a little desperate to find out what's going on over there. Is Abby there yet?"

"No, she's still on her way." I grab a pad of paper and a pen out of a junk drawer in the kitchen and I head for the pantry to make a grocery list. I'll text it to Chris as soon as I'm off the phone.

"What are you planning to do with her? Just pretend like the last eighteen years never happened?"

"I can't erase the last eighteen years and, honestly, I don't want to. They've taken such good care of her, Senia. You have to come down for the bonfire next weekend. You have to see how beautiful she is. And she's so smart and… I just don't know what I'm going to do when she goes home."

"Oh, Claire. I'd hate to see you get your heart broken again."

I jot down a few missing items on my list, then I come out of the pantry and head for the kitchen sink. I gaze out the window at the waves breaking on the sand and I try to imagine what it would be like to lose Abby a second time. But I can't.

"I know it sounds crazy, but I think you have nothing to worry about. Just promise me you'll come for the bonfire on Saturday. I need to introduce Abby to her Aunt Senia."

"Oh, you slut. You made me cry."

After I end the call with Senia and text the grocery list to Chris, I lay my phone on the kitchen counter and step outside through the front door onto the porch overlooking the ocean. The sun has almost set, so the evening breeze is starting to pick up, lifting the hairs around my face. I admire the waves while I make a mental list of things I need to do to prepare for the bonfire.

"Mom?"

I spin around and Junior is standing in the doorway. "Yes?"

He smiles and steps outside, then he wraps his arms around my shoulders. "Just wanted to give you a hug."

He's already an inch taller than me, so I squeeze him around the waist as hard as I can. "You're getting so tall. Pretty soon you're going to leave me, too."

"I won't leave you, Mom." I squeeze him hard and he laughs. "I swear. I'm not going anywhere."

I let him go and Abby and Caleb are standing just inside the open front door. But she's not looking at Junior and me. She's mesmerized by the ocean. She steps outside slowly, her gaze fixed on the crashing waves.

I want to take her hand and wade out into the water with her, the way I used to do when the kids were too small to go in the ocean alone. But that would be awkward at her age. Wouldn't it?

I reach out my hand slowly and she stares at it for a moment before she takes it. "Come on. The water's very warm at this time of day."

She nods and we head down the long wooden ramp toward the beach, Caleb and Junior following closely behind us. The breeze gets cooler and the briny smell of the ocean gets stronger the closer we get to the shore. When we reach the water's edge, Junior and Caleb strip off their T-shirts and shoes, then they race into the waves in their shorts. Abby and I kick off our sandals and she looks a bit apprehensive about going into the water.

That's when I remember something someone once told me when I was a bit scared of the roaring surf at this beach.

"A good friend of mine once told me to pay attention to the rhythm and movement of the water. Once you figure out the pattern, it's not so scary."

I hold out my hand to her again and I'm surprised when she takes it. We head for the water, her in her shorts and me in my knee-length skirt. But the moment the water touches her feet, she yelps.

"Oh, my God. Something touched me!"

I chuckle as a piece of seaweed washes ashore next to her foot. "It's just seaweed. Are you okay?"

She laughs and steps away from the limp sea plant. "I'm fine."

We take a few more steps, until the water kisses the hem of my skirt. She yelps a few more times when some more seaweed gets tangled on her ankle. And I have to admit that I'm almost glad for the seaweed when she grabs onto my arm with both hands, as if I can protect her from the slimy plants.

With each tiny wave that crashes into our legs, I see her relax a little more. Until finally, she's gazing at

Junior and Caleb, who are about twenty yards farther in, and she smiles. "This is beautiful."

"This is *yours*, for as long as you want to stay here."

CHAPTER TWENTY

RYDER AND I come home to find everyone, except Jimi, sitting in the living room watching TV in their pajamas. They're all sporting damp hair, which tells me they must have gone to the beach then showered. Claire smiles and jumps off the sofa to greet us at the door. Caleb quickly removes his arm from around Abby and stands up.

"Do you need some help?" he offers, and I try not to look annoyed when I nod.

It makes no sense for me to be upset that Caleb is so important to Abby. It's not as if he's taking my little girl away from me. She was never mine, until she showed up at my house yesterday morning. I just can't shake this feeling that she's only here temporarily. And if she's sitting there, curled up on the couch watching TV, it should be my arm around her. Caleb will probably always have her, but this may be my only chance.

Once we get the groceries inside, Claire takes the pillows upstairs to get the freshly laundered linens on Abby's bed in Jimi's bedroom. Abby, Caleb, Ryder, and Junior head back to the living room to finish whatever they were watching, but I stop Caleb before he can leave the kitchen.

"We need to talk. Come with me."

Abby and Ryder look over their shoulders at Caleb as they continue toward the living room, both of them wearing a look of pity for poor Caleb. I watch as Ryder seizes the opportunity to sit next to Abby on the sofa and the sight takes my breath away. I might as well be dreaming. None of this feels real. Well, except for the unfortunate conversation I'm about to have with Caleb.

"Come on," I beckon him as I head toward the door on our right. The library.

The beach house isn't big enough for a studio, so I had the acoustic insulation installed inside the walls of the library and this is where we keep the baby grand piano and the guitars. I shut the door behind Caleb as he enters and his eyes are wide as he looks around the room.

Three of the four walls in the library are covered from floor to ceiling in bookshelves, which display Claire's enormous collection of books. The outside wall has two large bay windows with bench seats for reading nooks. The portion of wall between the two windows is covered in frames displaying gold and platinum albums. Right in front of that wall is the baby grand piano. Off to the left is a mahogany leather sofa; to the right are two leather armchairs. In the corner is a display of five different guitars on stands.

"This is amazing," Caleb remarks as he's pulled toward the guitars. "Is that a… Is that a '68 Stratocaster?"

I laugh at this. "Yes, it's a '68, but it's not the '68 Stratocaster you're thinking of. Not that I haven't tried offering the Allen family ridiculous sums of money for Jimi's Strat, but they aren't interested in money. Sit," I say, pointing at the sofa.

He swallows hard then heads over to sit down. "Is this about Abby? I didn't even realize I had my arm around her. I won't let it happen again."

I shake my head as I sit on the piano bench with

my back to the keys. "It's not about you having your arm around Abby's shoulders. This is about you…" *Oh, God help me.* "This is about you and Abby having sex… while you're here."

"No, sir. We don't plan on doing that. I swear. We haven't even had sex yet."

I hold up my hand so he doesn't go into further detail. "Okay, I believe you. I just want to make sure you know that I can't have that in my house. As much as I'd like to believe that Abby is my daughter, at this point, I'm just her steward. So while you two are here, it is my duty to make sure Abby doesn't do anything that she wouldn't do in her… her *other* parents' home. You understand?"

"Yes, sir. I understand."

"Good. You're excused."

He eyes me warily as he stands from the sofa as if I'm trying to trick him into turning his back on me. Once he's standing, he doesn't head for the door. He just stares at the guitars in the corner.

"Do you think it would be okay if I played it? Just to try it out?"

"The '68?"

He nods and a boyish grin spreads across his face. I shake my head as I stand from the piano bench and head over to grab the '68 Strat off its stand. I pick up the guitar and, since I'm already there, I grab my '59 Les Paul Standard. I tread carefully toward the sofa and hold out the '68. Caleb grabs the strap first, then he grabs the neck. We both plug into the amp, which stands on the floor between the piano and the guitars. Then he slings the strap over his head and across his back, looking pleased that he doesn't have to adjust the length.

I strap on my Les Paul and immediately begin tuning it. This goes on for a couple of minutes before I realize there's no sound coming from Caleb's guitar. I look up and he's just staring at me.

"Something wrong?"

"I can't believe I'm about to play with Chris Knight. Is that an original '59 Les Paul?"

I purse my lips at this question. "I don't do reissues. Is that thing tuned?"

"Oh, yeah."

He begins testing each string. After a few minor adjustments on the tuners, he nods at me. I nod back and I take the lead, playing the opening guitar solo of "Little Wing" by Jimi Hendrix with heavy overdrive. If Caleb can answer back on this song, then he will officially have my approval. By the second measure, I can see he knows what I'm playing. By the fifth measure, he joins in. We only make it to the eleventh measure before Ryder and Abby walk into the library smiling.

"I knew that was you!" Ryder says, pointing at me. "I want to play."

Abby gawks at Caleb, who's grinning from ear to ear. "You were playing, too?"

"We were until you interrupted us."

"Oh, well, don't mind me. Please continue your jam session."

"Where's your guitar?"

"Upstairs."

Caleb slips the guitar strap off and tightens it a bit before he holds it out to Abby. She shakes her head. She's being shy.

Ryder heads straight for the piano. He's been taking lessons with Rachel, my other best friend Jake's wife, for three years, but he prefers the guitar. So it's odd to see him choose the piano. He must have a particular song in mind.

I glance over at Abby and Caleb and they're both staring at Ryder. Then he plays the first note and I instantly know what it is. I walk over to stand behind him as he plays the opening to "Imagine" by John

Lennon. When the first verse starts, I sing along with him. By the third line, Caleb has joined us and Abby is giggling uncontrollably. Caleb doesn't have a very good singing voice, but what he lacks in talent, he makes up for in enthusiasm. At the first chorus, I play a soft accompaniment on my Les Paul while Caleb and Ryder continue singing. Abby sidles up to the piano, tapping her foot to the beat.

"Come on, Abby. You know you want to dance," Caleb says, and Ryder laughs as he continues playing. "Just do it. Dance like nobody's watching."

Caleb raises his arms above his head and does a little pirouette. Ryder laughs so hard he loses track of the melody.

Abby punches Caleb in the arm. "Shut up."

I beckon Abby to come closer. "Come here."

I nod toward Ryder and she sits next to him on the bench. He shows her how to tap out a single note while he plays on the other side of the keys. He starts singing the first line of the second verse, and my heart soars when she joins in on the next line. When the song is over, I notice Caleb is staring at her with the same starry look I'm probably wearing.

I guess John Lennon was right. We're all just a bunch of dreamers. And I hope we never wake up.

CHAPTER TWENTY-ONE

Abby

SHARING A BEDROOM with Jimi for six days has been beyond awkward. I almost left the beach house to go home on two different occasions this week.

The first time I felt like leaving happened on the first morning after we arrived on Sunday evening. When I went to bed on Sunday, Jimi pretended not to hear me enter the room, and I went straight to sleep. But the following morning, I was awakened by the sound of Jimi's alarm at six a.m. It took her at least a minute to turn off the incessant beeping. Then she scurried about the bedroom, banging closet doors and dresser drawers as she looked for something. I guess there wasn't enough light in the room, so she groaned and complained aloud, "Ugh. I can't see *anything* in here." Then she pulled the curtains wide open so the bedroom was flooded with light. The whole time, I kept trying to convince myself that I should throw off the covers and say something to her. Offer her some help finding whatever it was she was looking for. But I was just so angry. I was afraid I'd say something rude.

Caleb convinced me to stay when I told him what happened. And everything seemed fine the rest of the week. She hasn't spoken to me much, but she did show Caleb and me how to check the electrical breakers in the basement when the amp Chris let us borrow wasn't working when we plugged it into an outlet in the living room. Then last night, Jimi's friend Sydney arrived and I absolutely wanted to leave. Over a fairly uneventful family dinner, Jimi asked if I could sleep with Caleb in Ryder's room while Sydney was visiting for the weekend. Of course, I had no idea she was going to make this request. When I looked up at her from my plate of pasta, she was smiling at me.

"That's what you want, right? To sleep with Caleb?"

My heart pounded so hard with anger and shame, I had to take a Nitrostat. I wanted to pack up my stuff and leave right then. I went down to the basement to fetch my empty suitcase, but the sound of footsteps on the wooden stairs stopped me. I expected to see Caleb or even Chris or Claire. But when I turned to see who had followed me down, I was surprised to see Ryder descending the last few steps into the humid basement.

"Please don't go, Abby."

The disappointment in his wide brown eyes and the frown on his pink lips broke my heart. I was so tired. Physically and emotionally. But something inside me wanted to keep fighting for this little guy.

"It's a little more complicated than coming or going, Ryder. There's a lot of stuff going on underneath. Stuff that even I don't understand. And I don't want to hurt anyone. Including myself."

He stared at my black suitcase for a minute, then he looked up. "My dad said pain is what makes us stronger. If you stay, maybe your heart will get stronger and you won't have to take all that medicine."

I chuckled at this. "So you're saying I should tough it out? That it will be worth it in the end?"

He nodded at first, then he shrugged. "Does that mean you're staying?"

How could I say no when my eleven-year-old brother begs me to be strong for him? I put my suitcase back on the shelf and tried not to feel too guilty when Jimi opted to sleep on the sofa bed with Sydney last night. But I woke up this morning with a new resolve to endure and enjoy this summer with the Knights.

I'm in the kitchen helping Claire put together some trays of campfire foods: hot dogs, chicken skewers, and all the components for s'mores. Jimi and Sydney are at the grocery store picking up some more soda and napkins. Caleb is out on the beach helping Chris and the boys get the fire started. Tonight is the big bonfire where I get to meet more people who've been dying to meet me.

"Can you put some foil over that tray, sweetie?" Claire says, nodding at a tray of hot dog buns on the counter next to the kitchen sink.

I secure a couple of pieces of foil over the tray then turn back to her. "Can you remind me who I'm meeting today? I don't want to forget their names."

"Oh, don't worry about forgetting their names. They've had eighteen years to remember yours. No one's going to get upset if you don't have their name down on the first day."

I take a deep breath as I tuck my hands into the pockets of my jean shorts. "Well, do you think you can tell me what happened to… to your mom?"

Her back is to me as she grabs some tongs out of a drawer on the kitchen island, but for a moment she's frozen. Then she sets the tongs down on the cutting board in front of her and slowly closes the drawer. When she turns around, she's wearing a faint smile that just barely hides the pain in her eyes.

"I'm sorry. I didn't mean to upset you. I just wondered why I'm not going to get to meet her."

She lets out a regretful sigh. "Oh, she would have loved to meet you. I'm sure of that." She pauses for a moment and I consider telling her to forget I asked, but she finally looks up and her eyes focus on mine. "My mother died of a self-induced drug overdose when I was seven years old. She… She took her own life. She had a very difficult childhood and she just couldn't hang on any longer. But there's not a day that goes by when I don't wish she could have been stronger for me. But…" She smiles a bit to herself. "I may have never met Chris and your Grandma Jackie if my mother had been stronger. Jackie Knight took me into her home when I was fifteen. I had no home. No family. No friends. I had nothing. Jackie gave me all those things and more. She's an incredible woman and the kids adore their grandma. I can't wait for you to meet her. And Joel, too."

"Did somebody say my name?"

We both turn toward the hallway and a man with a gray beard and full head of gray hair is holding out his arms for Claire.

"Hey, Grandpa!" Claire says, hurrying to him to give him a big hug.

A woman with short, stylish auburn hair squeezes around them. "Where's—"

She sees me before she can finish her sentence and I have a feeling she was going to ask for me. Her brown eyes widen and I can see the resemblance between her and Chris. Yes, I have her eyes.

"Oh, goodness," she whispers, raising her hands to cover her mouth. "Oh, my goodness. Look at you."

My stomach is wound into a tight ball of nerves as she watches me in silence, tears spilling over her ample cheeks, streaking her makeup. I don't know if I should say something or go to her. This isn't quite as awkward as when I first met Chris and Claire one week ago. Chris and Claire have been sharing some stories about Grandma Jackie with Caleb and me this week, prepping us for this reunion. But it's still pretty strange. She looks nothing like my mom's mom, Nana Bea. Grandma Jackie has style for a woman in her mid-sixties.

The man with the beard comes up behind her and looks at me as he gently grasps her shoulders. "I take it you're the famous Abigail everyone's been talking about?"

"Yes, sir. That's me."

"Oh, that voice!" She throws up her hands as if she simply can't take it anymore, then she comes to me. "Aren't you just the prettiest thing this side of heaven?"

She holds out her arms and I step forward to give her a hug. The way she hugs me almost makes me want to cry: her arms coiled tightly around my shoulders, her hand clasped around the back of my skull as I slowly lower my head onto her shoulder. She smells so good, like lavender and cake icing.

"Oh, honey. Not a day has gone by that I haven't wondered about you. I'm so happy you came to us. I hope you don't mind if I just hold on to you the whole night. Do you mind?" We all laugh and she squeezes me tighter. "Oh, all right. I guess we can let your Grandpa Joel have a crack at you." She lets go slowly, planting a kiss on my forehead as she grips my shoulders in her soft hands. "You look just like your daddy."

I smile and glance at Claire, who's shaking her

head in dismay as tears roll down her cheeks. "Hey, Grandma. How about giving Grandpa his turn?"

"Yes, let me greet this young lady properly."

Jackie steps aside and Joel steps forward. He gives me a quick hug, but it's enough to make my neck itch from his scratchy beard. Jackie and Joel help Claire and me take all the food out to the beach, where Chris and the boys have a roaring fire burning. Surrounding the fire pit are an eclectic assortment of beach chairs and a couple of drink coolers.

Jimi and Sydney return about twenty minutes later with the sodas and a guy who introduces himself as Sydney's boyfriend, Jace. He and Sydney actually look alike. They both have the same shade of dark-brown hair with golden caramel highlights. They're both about six feet tall with golden tanned skin. Next to five-foot-nine Jimi with her barely sun-kissed skin and bouncing light-brown hair, they all look practically perfect.

Over here on this side of the fire pit, Caleb is leaning back in his beach chair with his baseball cap on backward and his tattoos illuminated by the flickering firelight. I glance a few chairs to my left at Chris, and his tattoos. Glancing to my right, I catch Jackie gazing at me adoringly. And I realize that Caleb and I fit in here just as much as Jimi and her friends do, maybe even more. Maybe that's why she feels so threatened by me?

As I watch Jimi and her friends head toward the water, I breathe a sigh of relief. Feeling like I may have this situation just a little more figured out.

A few minutes later, Claire's friend Senia arrives with her husband, Tristan, and their two girls, Sia and Izzy. Senia is as tall as her husband and she looks like she fits in with Jimi and her friends. But she doesn't act anything like Jimi. She greets me with a bone-crushing hug and a drawing from Izzy to me.

Senia holds my arms as she looks me in the eye. "You may not remember this, but I watched you being born." I laugh at this and she hugs me again. "You're so pretty."

"Mom?" Senia finally lets go and we look down to find Izzy looking up at us. "Did she like it?"

Eight-year-old Izzy reminds me of a tiny version of Jimi, with her wide gray eyes and long light-brown hair that curls at the ends. Her older sister, Sia, is thirteen and looks almost exactly like Senia, but she's a bit less outgoing. And I can tell she's a total daddy's girl when I see Tristan take her aside so they can have a private discussion.

Izzy pretends to gaze at the fire as I examine the drawing she gave me. "Thank you, Izzy. I love it so much."

She glances at me and flashes me a shy smile as she shrugs. Then Claire comes over to see the drawing and I'm tempted to try and hide it, but I can't.

"Let me see," she says, holding out her hand.

I hand her the drawing and she blinks her eyes to keep the tears from falling. It's clearly a drawing of me with blonde hair and a broken heart drawn on my chest. Standing behind me are a blonde woman and a man with dark hair and tattoos all over his arms. The weird thing is that I could put this up in my bedroom at home and say it's a drawing of me with my mom and Caleb, but it's clearly a picture of me with Chris and Claire.

Claire looks up at me and smiles. "Izzy is an angel." She comes up behind Izzy and wraps her arms around her shoulders as she plants a smacking kiss on her cheek. "Beautiful drawing, baby."

"Hey, how about me?" Ryder says. "I'm an angel, too." He sticks his index fingers in his dimples as he grins.

Claire lets go of Izzy and shakes her head. "If you're an angel, we're all going to heaven."

Ryder pumps his fist in the air. "Yeah!"

Joel rises from his chair and grabs a few beers out of the cooler. He holds one out to Claire as she takes a seat next to Chris again.

She glances at Chris before she shakes her head. "No, thank you."

"Come on, pumpkin. Let loose. This is a time to celebrate."

She chuckles, her gaze fixed on her hands where they lie in her lap. "I'm fine. Thank you, Joel."

Joel shrugs as he heads back to his chair. "More for me."

Claire continues to stare at her hands, looking very uncomfortable. I turn to Jackie and she's staring at Claire with that same wide-eyed expression she had when she saw me in the kitchen.

"Claire Brooklyn Knight, do you have something you want to tell us?"

Claire looks up at Jackie, appearing as if she just got caught with her hand in the cookie jar, as my Nana Bea would say. "What do you mean?"

"Oh, don't you play coy with me, young lady. Are you two keeping something from me… again?"

Claire turns to Chris and he raises his eyebrows, as if he can't believe what's happening. "Jesus, Mom. Can we have a bonfire without—" Jackie casts a vicious glare in his direction. "Claire's pregnant."

"Chris!" Claire yelps.

"What? She was giving me the look. You know I hate the look."

Claire smacks his knee, then she leans forward and buries her face in her hands.

"Is it true, Mom?" Ryder shouts at her over the sound of the crackling fire.

Claire is silent for a moment, then she sits up straight and looks straight at Jackie. "Yes, it's true. We just found out a week ago, so it's still very early. We were going to keep it a secret until I was in the second trimester, but yes, it's true. I'm pregnant. Again."

"Jeez, Mom. *Five* kids?" Junior calls out across the fire pit with a chuckle.

"Six!" Caleb says, raising his hand, and everyone laughs. "In-laws count, right?"

"Are you two *married*?" Chris roars.

"No!" Caleb and I shout at the same time.

"He was just kidding!" I shriek, smacking his arm. "You jerk."

Ryder jumps out of his chair and points at Chris. "You were only twenty-one when you married Mom."

Junior laughs so hard at this, he's clutching his

belly when he points at Claire. "And *you* were knocked up with Jimi when you got married."

"Junior! Go to your room."

"What?" Junior howls, pointing his thumb at Ryder. "Why doesn't *he* have to go to his room?"

"Both of you go to your room!" Claire shouts.

"Oh, come now, honey. You can't fault the boys for stating the facts," Jackie says, barely hiding her smile.

Caleb leans over and whispers in my ear, "Best family reunion ever."

His lips on my ear give me the chills and I wish I could just take him in my arms and make out with him. We haven't made out in a week and I'm starting to get antsy. I miss his kiss. And his touch. I don't know how much longer I can hold out here before this summer begins to suck.

But Caleb is right. This bonfire has definitely been the highlight of this evening, and possibly the whole summer. And now I have another brother or sister on the way. One who will know me from the day he or she is born.

Best. Reunion. Ever.

CHAPTER TWENTY-TWO

Caleb

ABBY IS SITTING on the edge of her rollaway bed in Jimi's bedroom in her blue and white pajamas, frantically digging through her purse. I don't know what she's looking for, but when I see her pull out all her meds, two amber bottles and one box of Nitrostat, I know something is wrong. One of the bottles looks empty.

Jackie and Joel left to stay at an inn down the road and Jimi is sleeping downstairs with Sydney again until Sydney leaves tomorrow. Chris and Claire and the boys are in their rooms getting ready for bed, but I'm sure Chris or Claire—probably Chris—will be checking in on us shortly to make sure I don't try to sleep in here with Abby.

"I don't know what happened to my extra bottle of Xarelto. I thought I packed it," Abby says, upending her purse so all its contents fall out into a pile on the bed. She continues sifting through the six different lip balms and three different makeup compacts, but there are no more medicine bottles.

Abby has to take Xarelto, a blood thinner, to keep blood clots from forming in her heart. Because of her heart valve disease, blood can sometimes pool inside her heart. If she doesn't take the Xarelto, clots can form, travel through her blood vessels and into her brain, and cause a stroke. With this new form of Xarelto, she only has to take it twice a week. But taking the pills less often means there's less room for error if she forgets to take one or if she runs out of her meds in the evening. Which is why all her prescriptions are filled at 24-hour pharmacies.

"Give me that bottle. I'll call the pharmacy in Raleigh and tell them to transfer the prescription to another 24-hour pharmacy over here."

"But they won't fill the prescription twice in one month. It's a ninety-day supply."

"They will if you tell them you're out of town and you left your meds at home. Then, when you go home and find the bottle you were supposed to pack, you'll have a 180-day supply. Less trips to the pharmacy and problem solved."

She hands me the empty Xarelto bottle and I quickly dial the number for the CVS pharmacy listed on the label. I'm on the phone with the pharmacy technician for no more than five minutes before they have the prescription transferred to a 24-hour CVS in Wilmington.

"See? All fixed. Now we just have to tell your parents we're leaving at ten o'clock at night."

Abby starts dumping everything back into her purse. "They'll understand. Go wait outside. I have to change."

I smile as I head out into the dark hallway and realize I'm finally going to have a chance to get Abby alone for a few minutes. This past week, not being able to touch her and kiss her anytime I want, has been pure torture. She's my sunshine and the past seven days have been plagued by heavy overcast.

She comes out of the bedroom in her shorts and a tank top just as Chris comes out of the bedroom in a T-shirt and pajama pants. "What's going on?" He looks at Abby's hand and that's when I notice the empty pill bottle she's holding. "Are you sick? Do you need to go to the hospital?"

"No," she replies quickly, holding up the bottle. "I'm just out of my meds. Caleb is taking me to the 24-hour CVS in Wilmington. We should be back soon. Is that okay?"

"Of course. Yeah, go ahead. Go get whatever you need. Do you need any cash? Hold on, I'll go get my wallet."

"No, it's fine. The meds are free."

"Are you sure? You're not just saying that?"

She chuckles as she tucks the bottle into her purse. "I'm positive. It's part of the disability benefits. I… We should get going. We'll be right back."

And on that awkward note, Abby pulls me down the stairs and through the back door to the driveway, where my car is parked. Once we're inside, I lower the top so we can feel and smell the cool sea breeze and she heaves a sigh of relief.

"How awkward, to have to explain to my millionaire dad that I collect disability benefits."

"It's not a big deal," I say, backing the 'Cuda out onto Sandpiper Street. "I'm sure he probably figured as much considering you were born with that condition."

"Still, it doesn't make it any less weird."

I reach across and squeeze her thigh as I head toward Lumina. "It's okay, Abby. I'm sure it was way more weird for him than it was for you. Imagine knowing that your child was on disability because her adoptive parents wanted nothing to do with you. He's probably feeling like a jerk for not being more persistent about being a part of your life."

"And probably pissed that my parents wouldn't let him help me. God, they really screwed this up."

I turn left on Lumina, then I hop onto Highway 74. We pull into the CVS parking lot on Market Street about twenty minutes later. We rush inside and head straight for the pharmacy counter in the back. The pharmacist working is an Asian lady with a pleasant smile.

"May I help you?" she asks, flashing us a friendly smile when we approach the pickup counter.

"Yes, my prescription was just transferred here about thirty minutes ago. For Abigail Jensen."

She furrows her perfectly shaped eyebrows together and shakes her head. "I haven't gotten anything for that name in the last half hour, but I'll double-check."

She checks through the alphabetized bags hanging from the stack of rods behind her. She sifts through the A's and the J's twice before she comes back empty-handed.

"I'm sorry. I don't have anything here under that name. Let me just check the computer. Give me a moment."

She begins typing on the computer and I clasp my hand around the back of Abby's neck as we wait. I massage her a little, trying to help her stay calm as the pharmacist's fingers fly across the keyboard. Finally, she picks up her phone and dials a phone number.

"Hi. Yes, this is Karen Chen at 3822. Can you please verify that you have a prescription for forty milligrams of Xarelto for an Abigail Jensen? Please call us back as soon as you get this message."

My heart sinks when I realize she's leaving a voicemail. "No, you have to get that prescription. She needs it," I insist as she sets the phone down.

"I'm sorry, but they must have transferred your prescription to the wrong pharmacy. And the one they transferred it to closed at ten. It's almost eleven. You'll have to wait until they open at eight a.m. to pick it up over there."

"She can't wait until tomorrow!" I reply, leaning over the counter to try to see what her computer says. "She's only supposed to take it on Fridays and

Saturdays. Tomorrow's Sunday. She needs it now."

"Caleb, it's fine," Abby says, pushing me away from the counter. "Thank you for your help."

"You can't skip that pill until Friday. That's dangerous."

"It's fine. We'll pick it up tomorrow morning and I'll call my doctor and ask if I can take it on Sunday instead. No big deal."

I shake my head as she drags me out of the pharmacy and back to the car. Once we're inside, I realize we're going to be returning to the beach house without Abby's meds. They're probably going to think we were lying about the prescription so we could get out of the house.

By the time we get home, all the lights are off except for the glow of Sydney's cell phone where Jimi and Sydney are huddled on the sofa bed. We bid them goodnight, then I take Abby to Jimi's room. I close the door behind me, pissed that the pharmacy tech in Raleigh must have misunderstood when I told her we were in Wrightsville Beach. She must have thought I wanted the prescription transferred to the CVS in Wrightsville Beach.

"I fucked up. I'm sorry."

"Oh, please. It's not a big deal. We'll go to the

pharmacy tomorrow morning." She stares at me for a moment, then she waves toward the bedroom door. "You have to go before they catch you in here."

I step forward and take her face in my hands, then I lay a tender kiss on her lips. I can hear her breathing quicken, so I lean in for another. She tastes like the fancy whitening toothpaste Jimi has in her bathroom. I slide my tongue into her mouth and she lets out a soft whimper.

"God, I've missed this."

She pushes me back a little, but her eyes are fixed on my mouth. "You have to leave. We can't do this here."

I lean over and kiss the tip of her nose. "I know, but I'm not leaving. I'm sleeping in here to watch over you."

"What? You can't sleep in here."

She attempts to push me toward the door, but I dig my heels in and I'm too solid for her to move. "If you're not taking all your meds tonight, I'm staying in here to watch over you whether you like it or not. I'll sleep on the floor."

She glares at me, but there's a hint of a smile curling the left side of her mouth. "Fine. But if anyone walks in here you have to hide."

"Oh, yeah. That's totally going to work. If anyone walks in here, we'll just tell them the truth. I stayed in here to make sure you were okay. If they have a problem with that, then screw them. Your health should be their number-one priority while you're staying here."

She shakes her head as she opens up the bottom drawer of Jimi's dresser, which Jimi cleared out for Abby to store her clothes. She grabs a T-shirt and pajama pants then clutches them to her chest while she stands silently contemplating something.

"You want me to turn around?" I know she's going to say yes, but I have to at least give her the option to try something new.

"No," she mutters.

"Really? I mean, are you sure?"

She looks up at me as she tosses the pajamas onto the rollaway bed. "Yes. I'm sure."

She pulls off her tank top and I try not to smile too wide when I see her white bra and the soft curve of her breasts. I've seen her in a bra before, but it was in the heat of the moment, with our bodies pressed against each other. Not like this, with her standing before me, her body on display.

She reaches up and lightly touches her fingertips to

the six-inch scar over her breastbone.

I step forward, keeping my eyes focused on hers as I pull her hand away from her chest. "You're gorgeous. Every inch of you."

She lowers her head as she reaches behind her back to unclasp her bra. "You don't think my boobs are too small?"

She slowly slips the bra straps off her shoulders and her breathing quickens as she peels it off and tosses it onto the bed next to her tank top.

"Too small?" I reply, unable to take my eyes off her slightly pink nipples. "No way. They're perfect."

She chuckles as she reaches for her pajama shirt. She pulls it on, then she undoes her shorts and shrugs out of them. Her skin has a bit of a bronze sheen from spending this week on the beach. I've seen her in her one-piece bathing suit almost every day since we came here, but something about watching her change in front of me feels more intimate.

She pulls on her pajama pants and throws her clothes in the hamper before she gets in under the covers. "I know it's a small bed, but I don't know where the spare blankets are for you to sleep on the floor. So I guess you'll have to sleep with me."

"Are you sure?"

"Of course," she replies, scooting over and patting the mattress for me to lie down with her.

I turn off the lamp and slide into bed with her. The bed squeaks under my weight, and for a moment I worry that this will wake someone up. But then Abby snuggles up to me with her head on my shoulder and her arm draped over my belly, and all my worries disappear.

I kiss the top of her head and give her shoulder a light squeeze. "Goodnight, sunshine."

"Goodnight, turtledove."

CHAPTER TWENTY-THREE

I OPEN MY EYES and the first thing I see is Caleb's black T-shirt. I smell his warm skin through the fabric. When I look up, I'm not surprised to find Caleb is wide awake and watching me.

"How long have you been awake?"

"About an hour. I didn't want to wake you up until 7:30 'cause we don't have to go to CVS until eight."

"Are you saying I need all the beauty rest I can get?" I say as I push myself up onto my elbow.

"Exactly what I'm saying. Look at you. You're hideous with that blonde hair tumbling over your graceful neck, highlighting the exquisite bone structure of your hideous visage."

I shake my head as I sit up, but the bed is too narrow for me to sit cross-legged. "Is everyone else awake? You should go back to Ryder's room."

He chuckles at my suggestion as he sits up. "You know that boy is still asleep, but everyone else is awake. I heard Claire and Jimi arguing. Anyway, there's no hiding this. Someone's going to see me coming out of this room."

"Wait. Aren't they supposed to go to a music festival at Carolina Beach today?"

Caleb's emerald eyes light up. "You're right. And your mom said you couldn't go."

I roll my eyes at this. When I called my mom yesterday morning, I told her how the Knights were taking me to a music festival in Carolina Beach. She told me I couldn't go because there would be too many people and I could easily overheat or get sick. Heart valve disease makes me more susceptible to endocarditis, an infection of the heart lining, vessels, or valves. I had endocarditis after the last surgery to reshape one of my leaflets, and my mom claims I almost died. Not that I don't believe her, but I've come to realize that my mom will say just about anything to make me do what she wants.

Since endocarditis is caused by bacteria that enter

the bloodstream, the chances of me getting it just by being around a bunch of people is ridiculous. But, as it is, she's already overly skittish about me swimming at the beach in that "nasty" ocean water. I don't want to press my luck by insisting on going to the music festival. Or she may drive down here herself and kidnap me.

"Well, I guess that means we have the house all to ourselves today," I say, looking over my shoulder at him.

"Don't get any ideas, Abby. I plan on holding onto my purity until my wedding night."

"What about that girl you had sex with before we started going out? The one who tried to break us up. What was her name again? Bitch whore slut?"

"Abby!" He clutches his chest, pretending to be appalled. "That is one dirty mouth you've got there. Are you sure you're a virgin?"

"As sure as I am that you're going to try to feel me up today."

He nods. "You're pretty sure."

"Should we go down there and have breakfast with them? Or should we just wait until they're gone?"

Caleb swings his legs over the side of the bed and I feel a twinge of guilt to see him still in his T-shirt and jeans. "I wonder why they haven't come in to check on us."

"Maybe they don't want to wake us? Maybe they figured you slept in here so you wouldn't wake Ryder last night when we got back from the pharmacy? *Maybe* they're actually cooler than we thought?"

As soon as I say this, we hear footsteps coming up the stairs. The footsteps pass right by Jimi's closed bedroom door and continue down the hallway toward Ryder's room. Junior yells at Ryder to get up and get his swimsuit on. They're leaving early so they can find a place to set up their stuff on the beach.

"Let's just wait until they're gone," Caleb whispers. "Then we can go to CVS and come back."

I nod and sit perfectly still for fifteen minutes until they've all left the house. I shower in Jimi's bathroom while Caleb uses the shower downstairs. Then we set off to the pharmacy. Once I have my prescription in hand, I dial my cardiologist's emergency phone number and leave a message asking if it's okay for me to take the pill on a Sunday.

"So what do you want to do today? Want to go swimming?" Caleb yells at me to be heard over the roaring rush of wind in our ears as we fly down Highway 74.

I tuck my skirt under my legs, then I close my eyes and the wind washes over my face, coaxing the moisture out the corners of my eyes and making my skin feel stale and tight.

"I want to stay in," I shout back at him.

When we get home, I see I have a voicemail message from my cardiologist, Dr. Rosenthal. I get out of the car and listen to the message as Caleb puts up the ragtop.

"Good morning, Abby. This is Dr. Rosenthal. I received your message and I'd rather have you skip the dose than take it a day late. Just try not to engage in any strenuous activity this week and call 911 immediately if you have any symptoms of a blockage, such as numbness, speech problems, severe headache, or loss of balance. Hope you're enjoying your summer at the beach. It's important for a young girl such as yourself to have some fun. See you next month, Abby."

"What did he say?" Caleb asks as we climb the steps to the back door.

"He said not to worry about taking it today."

"Really?"

"Yeah, and he said it's important for a young girl such as myself to have some fun."

Caleb laughs as we enter the cool air-conditioned living room. "I guess we know what that means."

"What does that mean?"

Caleb closes the back door then looks at me as if I should know the answer to this question. "Hel-*lo*? Monopoly!" He grabs my waist and pulls me close. "I'll be the race car. You can be the thimble."

I lay my hands on his chest and my stomach flips as he gazes down at me with a hungry look in his eyes. "So, because I'm a woman I have to be the thimble? How sexist. Now I want to be the boot so I can kick your race car in the—"

"Whoa there! No need for violence."

He leans down and plants a soft kiss on my lips. I reach up, curling my arms around his neck so I can return the gesture with a bit more passion. His lips are so smooth and kissable. I suck on his top lip and he groans softly into my mouth. Then something prods my thigh and I realize it's the erection growing inside his cargo shorts.

I pull my head back to look at him. To let him know that I can feel how much he wants me. And that I want him just as much.

"I love you, Caleb."

"I love you more, sunshine."

He gazes into my eyes, his nostrils slightly flared as he slowly bends his knees and scoops me up into his arms. My heart races the second my feet leave the ground, but Caleb has carried me in his arms plenty of times. I'm not afraid he'll drop me. I'm nervous about what's going to happen when he puts me down.

He kisses my forehead, then he sets off up the stairs. He pushes Jimi's door open with his foot and I feel a strange urge to giggle as he gently lays me down on the rollaway bed. Am I really going to lose my virginity on a creaky rollaway bed?

He lays half his body on top of mine and the other half on the bed. I press my lips together to keep from laughing.

"Are you nervous?" he asks, brushing my hair out of my eyes.

"Are we really going to do this?"

"Do what?"

I let out a nervous giggle. "This." I look down at the place where his hips are lying on top of mine.

He looks confused. "What do you mean? We've done this plenty of times. Did you—" A smile spreads across his face. "Did you think I was bringing you up here to have sex?"

"You weren't?"

He chuckles softly. "No, but now that we're talking about it… Is that what you want?"

"Here?"

"Anywhere."

My heart is starting to pound painfully against my chest. "Maybe I should take a Nitro before we talk about this."

"Good idea."

He jumps off the bed and we both kick off our shoes as he grabs my purse off the dresser. He sets it down on the bed and watches as I pop a small white tablet under my tongue. Once it's dissolved, I hand him back my purse and he sets it down on the dresser. When he turns around, his eyes are closed. I wait a few seconds, but he just stands there.

"Caleb, what's wrong?"

He opens his eyes and the muscle in his jaw twitches as he grits his teeth together, but the tears begin to fall despite his best efforts. I've never seen Caleb cry. Not even when his father died. I've seen him get down and I once saw him so angry with his life that I feared he might hurt himself. But I've never seen him cry. And just the sight of it scares me and instantly brings tears to my eyes.

"It's not fair that you have to take medicine just to

talk about something that other people take for granted. You deserve better, Abby. You deserve a real heart that's just as strong as your figurative heart."

He sits on the bed next to me and I sit up on my knees so I can wrap my arms around his neck. He pulls me into his lap and buries his face in my neck.

"I don't want to lose you," he says, his voice thick with emotion. "I don't know what I'd do without you. You're all I have left."

"I'm not going anywhere, Caleb."

We hold each other for a while in silence, just breathing each other in, one slow breath after the other. Every once in a while, I plant a kiss on his jaw and he responds by squeezing me a bit tighter. Finally, I tilt my head back to look at his face and he's not crying anymore, but his eyes are still a little red.

"I want to have sex… here."

His eyebrows perk up. "Now?"

I sniff loudly as I nod. "Yes, now."

He reaches up and his gaze is fixed on my mouth as he brushes the backs of his fingers over my cheek. "I don't want to hurt you. Will you promise to tell me if I hurt you?"

"Of course."

He slides his hand behind my neck and pulls my

mouth to his. His tongue pushes forward, parting my lips, and I let out a soft sigh. His breath is hot in my mouth as I curl my fingers in his hair and suck on his tongue.

I pull my head back as I slide my lips down to the length of his tongue. Opening my eyes slowly, I smile when I see the surprised look on his face. I chew on my bottom lip and wait for him to say something. Instead, he takes me in his arms and flips me onto my back.

I giggle a little, but the nervous laughter quickly goes away when he rests both hands on either side of my head and leans down to kiss me. He kisses me slowly as his hips rock gently back and forth. With each stroke of his tongue and each slow thrust of his pelvis, the throbbing sensation between my legs intensifies.

One of his hands slides down between us and slowly gathers up my skirt until his hand is cupping my mound and I am so glad I took a Nitrostat or I'd be having a heart attack right now. I wonder if he can feel my flesh pulsating against his fingers as he gently strokes me through the cotton fabric of my panties.

He pulls his head back to look me in the eye as he touches me. His eyes light up as my mouth drops open and I suck in a sharp breath. He continues to stroke me softly until I'm panting heavily.

The bedroom door flies open and Caleb and I sit up quickly as Jimi storms in, no apology for interrupting us.

"Um... excuse me, but we kind of wanted some privacy," I say, pulling my skirt down as I swing my legs over the side of the bed.

She glances at me then continues searching through her desk for something. "Um, excuse me, but I'm not the one who said you had to share a room with me. If you want some alone time to bone each other, maybe you should take it up with your parents."

Jimi grabs a set of keys out of her desk drawer then turns on her heel to leave. I can feel Caleb looking at me, but I'm too stunned to move or speak. She hates me. She isn't just threatened by me. She truly hates me.

It takes me a whole eight minutes to get my black suitcase out of the basement and get all my stuff packed up. All the while, Caleb just watches me in silence.

"You're not even going to wait until they get back to say good-bye to them? You're not even going to think about this, Abby?"

"Think about it? You want me to *think* about it?

All I've done this week is think about why someone who has *everything* could envy someone who has *nothing*. I don't even have my *health*, and she still thinks it's okay to treat me as if I'm some princess who rode in and dethroned her."

"You have nothing? What the fuck am I? Who the fuck are all the other people in this house who love you as if they've always known you? Do you call that nothing?"

"I don't want to talk about this," I say as I try to drag my suitcase off the bed and it ends up falling on my foot. "Shit! Just take me home."

"I'm not taking you anywhere until you calm down."

"Fine. I'll go without you."

CHAPTER TWENTY-FOUR

Caleb

I FOLLOW ABBY out of the bedroom, down the stairs, and out the front door to the beach. We trudge through the hot sand in our bare feet, straight toward the water, not saying anything. When we're far enough from the beach house, I finally ask the question that Abby needs to consider.

"How many times do you think Jimi has imagined what it would be like when you came back into her parents' lives?" She turns when we reach the water's edge so we're walking parallel to the shore, but she doesn't reply. "She's probably thought about it a lot. She's had years to think about it. She's lived most of her life contemplating what it would be like. Don't you think that at some point, she realized there was a chance things could go wrong? That the moment you arrived, she would no longer be Daddy and Mommy's only girl? She would no longer be special."

"Her pain doesn't invalidate mine, Caleb. Nice try, though."

"I'm not implying that her feelings make your feelings invalid. All I'm saying is that you're both entitled to have those feelings."

"Does that also mean she's entitled to treat me like a hobo? Like I'm here because I have nowhere else to go?" She stops walking and rounds on me. "I have a home with parents who love me. I don't *have* to be here! I can leave whenever I want."

"Which is exactly what she wants."

"Oh, please spare me the 'if you leave, Jimi wins' speech. I'm a little too old to fall for that. This isn't a competition to see who wins."

"Just because it's not a competition to you, it doesn't mean that's not exactly how Jimi sees it."

"Ugh." She throws up her hands then spins around and continues traipsing through the damp sand, while the families on the beach look at her as if she's crazy. "If she wants to play a game she's guaranteed to win, she should just challenge me to some *strenuous activity*."

She puts air quotes around *strenuous activity* and I realize it's not just Jimi that's getting to her. She's also angry that Jimi interrupted us when we were about to have sex.

I grab her hand and dig my feet into the sand to stop her. "Abby, there will be plenty more times for us to do what we were about to do. It doesn't have to happen now. It doesn't have to happen this year. But it will happen, eventually. And when it happens," I take her face in my hands and kiss the tip of her nose, "it will happen somewhere where no one can interrupt us. God *damn it*, Jimi. Hey, want to go back and plant a rubber snake under her pillow?"

She shakes her head at my attempt to make light of the situation. "Okay, fine. I get it. I'm not going to let her get to me anymore. And I'll stay… on one condition."

I swipe my thumb across her bottom lip as I admire how beautiful she looks with the sunlight in her hair. "What condition?"

She puckers her lips to kiss the pad of my thumb, then she flashes me a smile so seductive it's practically indecent. "I want to have sex today."

I chuckle. "You drive a hard bargain, Abby." I kiss the corner of her mouth and she turns her face so she can kiss me on the lips, but I pull back a little. "Wait a minute. Where exactly do you plan on having sex? Jimi's probably still at the house. And even if she's gone, the rest of the family's getting home soon."

She smiles as she coils her arms around my neck and pulls me closer, her eyes glued to my mouth. "I was thinking we could do it right here."

"Right here? On the sand? With all these people around us? Is that your idea of family entertainment?"

She tightens her hold on my neck, then she jumps up and I catch her as she wraps her legs around my hips. "Take me into the water." She leans her forehead against mine and whispers, "I trust you."

CHAPTER TWENTY-FIVE

FOR ONCE, CALEB doesn't ask me if I'm sure this is what I want. He can see the certainty in my eyes and hear it in my voice. He puts me down momentarily so he can peel off his shirt and throw it onto the sand. Then, he picks me up again and I lay my head on his shoulder as he wades into the small waves with me in his arms.

I have to keep reminding myself every few seconds to keep breathing. Once he's a little higher than waist deep in the ocean, the water evens out. I tilt my head back to look at him, pressing my lips together to hide my enormous grin. He smiles back at me, but I'm pretty sure he's just as nervous as I am.

"Obviously, I've never done this," I begin, and this elicits a chuckle out of him. "But I'm thinking—"

He crushes his lips against mine before I can finish this sentence. His hand grasps the back of my head, tilting it sideways so our mouths are angled perfectly. He slides his tongue into my mouth and I moan as I feel his erection growing under the fabric of his shorts. He kisses me deeply until I'm out of breath, then he pulls away slowly.

"You think too much," he growls in my ear, and the gruffness in his voice sends a chill through me. "Loosen your grip on me. I'm gonna lay you back so you can get your hair wet."

I let go of his shoulders and he gently lays me back until the back of my head is submerged in the ocean. I smile at him as I pinch my nostrils and lean farther back so my whole head is under the water. I open my eyes and the saltwater stings, but after a few seconds my eyes adjust and I smile when I see Caleb's taut abdominal muscles rippling in the sunlight shining through the water.

Caleb pulls me up and I gasp for air. "What were you doing down there?" he asks, sounding a bit furious with me.

"Just enjoying the view."

He shakes his head and pulls my chest flush against his again. I wrap my arms around his neck and kiss him hard, allowing the saltwater on my tongue to mesh with the sweet minty taste of his. He keeps one arm coiled tightly around my waist as his other hand slides down between us and inside my panties.

"Oh, God," I whisper into his mouth.

His fingers explore me for a moment before he finds the spot he's looking for and my entire body twitches, as if I've been shocked. "Is that it?" he murmurs, tilting his head back to watch my face.

I nod and he smiles as he gently caresses me. My body continues to twitch involuntarily, so I grab the hair on the back of his head to steady myself. His finger glides softly over my sensitive flesh and I close my eyes so he can't see when they roll backward.

I throw my head back as my hips begin to rock back and forth on their own. He kisses my collarbone and I let out a brief whimper as my body yields to him. The orgasm rolls through me, every part of me spasming and twitching until it's over. It only lasts a few seconds, but I can honestly say those were the most amazing seconds of my life.

I lift my head and look Caleb in the eye as he removes his hand from inside my panties. I nod at him and his hand moves down to his shorts. I can't see what he's doing, but I imagine he's unbuttoning his shorts and pushing them down. Then I feel it. His erection springs up and touches my bottom. And it feels so hot.

I swallow hard as he grabs both sides of my waist and pushes me back a little. My legs are still wrapped around his hips as he reaches between my legs, pushes my panties to the side, and presses the tip of his erection against my opening. I try to look nonchalant, but inside I'm dying with excitement.

"Are you okay?"

"Yeah, I'm fine. Keep going."

One hand is on his erection, guiding himself inside me; his other arm is locked around my waist, holding me still, as he slowly enters me. He feels enormous, though I have no idea what it's supposed to feel like. I have nothing to compare him to.

His mouth falls softly over mine and I tighten my arms around his neck as he continues thrusting his hips slowly backward and forward, moving a bit farther inside with each thrust.

"Are you all the way in yet?"

He laughs and shakes his head. "Not even halfway."

"Oh, my God."

"Do you want me to stop?"

"No! No, please keep going."

He kisses my forehead then holds my gaze as he moves inside me. "Just relax and keep your eyes on mine, okay?"

I nod and he penetrates me deeper. I grit my teeth against the pain, keeping my eyes locked on his as he dances inside me. Until he's all the way in, and we're dancing together. Our hips move in unison, back and forth, up and down, inside and out. As if nobody's watching.

CHAPTER TWENTY-SIX

I RUSH DOWN THE back steps and find Sydney watching a video on her phone while sitting in the driver's seat of her silver convertible Audi R8. She laughs at something on her phone screen as I slide into the passenger seat, so I slam the door to get her attention.

"Can we please go?"

"Oh, my God. You have to see this video of Jared talking to his dog, Lola."

"I don't want to see the video. Just drive, please."

Her eyebrows shoot up as she drops her phone into the cup holder and pulls out of the driveway. "What's with the attitude? Did your parents call you Abby again?"

"No. And please don't remind me."

Sydney turns onto Lumina, holding the steering wheel steady with her knee as she pulls her wavy hair into a ponytail. The salty air swirls through my hair, whipping it around everywhere, but I don't care. I'm not trying to impress anyone today.

Sydney and I promised our friend Richard we'd watch him play a show at The Blue Fedora in Lumina Station this afternoon. He thinks my presence will attract more attention to the event, but I'm not in the mood for attention right now.

In fact, I really don't want anyone's attention, except my parents. But they're too busy pretending the past eighteen years never happened. And now my mom is pregnant again. How convenient. I'm sure Abby will be the perfect older sister. She'll change diapers and babysit and I'll be the selfish one who's too busy attending college on the other side of the country.

I can't wait until next year when I leave for California. Maybe then, with three thousand miles between us, I won't even notice that I've become invisible to my parents.

"You should just talk to your parents. You can say, 'Hey! Remember me? Your daughter who got accepted into every college she applied to?'" Sydney says as she stops at a red light.

"It wasn't every college," I mutter, pretending to be interested in the people sitting outside the café on the corner.

"Whatever. Seven out of eight is pretty fucking good, if you ask me. I got two out of nine, and that's only because you helped me on the UNC app."

"It doesn't matter. None of it matters to them right now. I could probably move to California a year early and my parents wouldn't even notice. But if I should wake up Queen Abby ten minutes too early, they'd probably take away my car or lock me away in the basement for the rest of the summer."

"You may be exaggerating a little bit now."

"They already took my phone! And they haven't even offered to give it back to me. I have no incentive to do anything for them right now."

I don't say it aloud, but the only time my parents have given me any attention since Abby arrived is when I've hurt her feelings. They didn't notice when I let her use my laptop to type up a letter to her academic counselor. They don't know that I've been going to bed way before I normally do so I don't keep her up. And without my phone, all I can do is lie there and think.

Mostly, I think about how everyone hates me right now. But I also think about how sorry I am that this reunion hasn't turned out better for all of us. I think about how I used to imagine getting a cool older sister who would teach me how to dress and wear my makeup, and how to talk to boys. It wasn't until she arrived that I realized that I can't count on Abby for any of those things. Because she's too much like my mom for me to ever relate to her.

I know some of the things I've said to Abby have crossed the line into malicious territory. But I'm just scared. My parents look at her and see the way I *should* have turned out: a mild-mannered musician, in a long-term relationship with a musician, going to a local college. When Abby leaves, they'll look at me and think, "Oh, well. At least one of our kids turned out right."

Nothing I do will ever compare to Abby's ability to tap into my parents' deepest emotions. No one can ever compare to the girl who got away.

Not even Ryder or Junior can compare to her, but it doesn't seem to bother them. Just thinking of this makes my stomach twist. My inability to compare to Abby is getting to me, and I've been unable to brush it off like my dumb younger brothers. What does that say about me?

"Turn around."

"What?"

"Turn the car around. I have to go back."

Sydney looks at me like I'm crazy. "Did you forget something?" I reach for the steering wheel and she bats my hand away. "Okay, okay! I'll turn around."

When Sydney pulls the convertible into the driveway, I'm relieved to see Caleb's car parked next to the garage. I tell Sydney to go home to Cary and I'll call her later. I race up the back steps and into the air-conditioned beach house.

"Abby!" I call out, but no one answers.

I dart up the stairs and into my bedroom. My chest aches when I see her black suitcase next to the rollaway bed. I check the rest of the house, but she and Caleb are nowhere. There's only one thing I can think to do right now. The only thing I think will show Abby that I'm done trying to prove a point.

I lift her suitcase onto my bed, then I carefully unpack all her belongings, putting everything back where it was. I put the suitcase back in the basement, then I strip the linens off the mattress and toss them into the washing machine. It takes me about forty minutes to figure out how to fold up the rollaway bed, and another ten minutes for me to haul it downstairs into the garage.

There's no way I can move the furniture in my room around by myself, but I'm sure my dad and Caleb can do that later. I pack up some of my clothes and shoes in a gym bag, tossing in the toiletries I keep in my private bathroom. Then I toss the bag onto the bottom bunk in Ryder's room. Finally, I grab all Caleb's stuff and move it out of Ryder's room and into mine. Then I write a note for Abby.

Abby,

I know the past week has been hard for you. It's been pretty hard for me, too. I thought I knew how I would feel when you got here. I thought I'd be happy to have an older sister. And, to be honest, when my mom first called me to tell me you came home, I was so happy I cried tears of joy.

But within seconds, those tears of joy turned into tears of grief for what I'd lost. When you arrived, I lost my status as the only girl. My dad's only princess. And instead of being honest with my parents, I decided to take it out on you. I hoped that if I made you feel bad enough, you'd leave and everything would go back to normal. But I was wrong. Nothing will ever be the way it was before you got here.

And I'm actually happy about that.

I've watched my parents suffer for too long. My dad doesn't know I know this, but he has been praying for you to come back to him for eighteen years. That's a long time to want something, or someone. I don't want to ruin this summer for you and especially not for them.

I'm sorry I tried to push you away. I'm sorry I wasn't the kind of sister or person you needed me to be.

I hope you'll accept this apology and my room for the rest of the summer.

Love,
Jimi

CHAPTER TWENTY-SEVEN

CALEB AND I manage not to piss off any beachgoers, but we agree that we'd better not stick around and press our luck. After our interesting dip in the ocean, we trudge back to the beach house in our wet clothes. Every time Caleb squeezes my hand, my stomach vaults as I remember how he moved inside me. Caleb was *inside* me! How weird and cool is that?

But as soon as the beach house comes into view, I suddenly remember what drove me out of there and onto the beach. I hope Jimi left with her friends. I really don't want to face her right now. She'll probably smell the sex on us and flash me a knowing smirk.

We use the outdoor shower to rinse off, then we sit on the wooden rocking swing on the porch for a while until we're no longer dripping. Every once in a while, we hear some movement inside the house. Jimi and her friend are probably enjoying the fact that I'm gone. Probably celebrating by dancing in their pj's.

"You ready to face the dragon?" Caleb says, wiggling his eyebrows.

"Can I use you as a human shield?"

"Yeah, baby. You know how much I like it when you use me."

I shove him and he laughs as I head for the front door. I enter the breakfast nook keenly aware of my bare feet and my damp salty clothes. If I can just avoid Jimi long enough to take a shower and put on some clean clothes, this will be much easier.

We practically tiptoe through the kitchen and the downstairs hallway, past the living room, and up the stairs to Jimi's bedroom. My heart clenches inside my chest when I see both my suitcase and the rollaway bed are gone. That must be what all the racket was inside the house when Caleb and I were on the porch. She must have been erasing all traces of my existence.

I cover my face and draw in a stuttered breath as the tears begin to fall. "Why does she hate me so much?"

Caleb takes me into his arms and strokes my hair. "Don't worry, sunshine. She just doesn't know you. And if she wants you out this bad, we'll leave tonight. Let's just wait for the rest of the family to get back so you can say good-bye."

"No, I want to leave now," I whisper, the pain in my chest spreading into my stomach, making me physically sick. "I can't do this anymore. If they don't understand why I had to leave, then I don't care. I don't want to have anything to do with them. Why?"

"Why what?"

"Why did I come here and put myself through this? Why did I think this would turn out well? Am I really that naive?"

Caleb holds my face in his hands and looks me in the eye. "You're not naive. You're just hopeful. You're like sunshine and she—"

"She what?"

He lets go of my face and squeezes past me, then he heads straight for Jimi's bed. He picks up a folded piece of light-blue notepaper off the comforter and stares at it for a moment before he turns around and holds it out to me.

"What is it?"

He shrugs. "I don't know, but it has your name on it."

I swipe my arm across my nose and take the paper from him. I unfold it slowly and my body aches with dread when I see my name written in Jimi's handwriting. But I swallow my fear and continue reading. By the time I read the last line, I'm a disgusting, weeping mess.

"What does it say?" Caleb whispers, pulling me into his arms but never trying to sneak a peek at the letter.

I dig my fists into his back as I hold on to him and cry into his damp T-shirt. "It's… it's an apology."

"Really?"

"Really."

I whip my head around at the sound of Jimi's voice and I'm surprised to see her standing in the threshold of her bedroom door, her eyes pink and puffy. She sniffs loudly as tears roll down her face.

"I'm sorry I was a jerk to you," she says, staring at the floor as she wipes the tears from her cheeks. "Please don't go. I promise I'll stop being a jerk. Just… please don't go yet. It would break my—our parents' hearts."

I let go of Caleb and I walk slowly toward her.

"I've never had a sister or brother. My mom told me that after what happened with my adoption, my parents were turned off on the whole process and they decided to not put themselves through it again. I think she told me that hoping it would influence my feelings toward my birth parents. Like I would blame them for the fact that I never had any siblings." I reach forward and take her hand in mine and she's still staring at the floor. "But I never felt that way. I knew that I didn't have siblings because my parents weren't strong enough to deal with the process. Not because my birth parents made it difficult. Just like I know... *our* parents aren't responsible for how you reacted to me coming here."

"They don't deserve to have this ruined for them. I was being selfish. I'm sorry. I just... I don't know how to be someone's little sister."

"I don't know how to be a big sister. But maybe we can learn together?"

She nods as she draws in a sharp, stuttered breath. I wrap my arms around her waist and I'm suddenly very aware of the fact that my little sister is at least three inches taller than me. She coils her arms around my shoulders tightly and it hurts my heart every time I feel her chest jerk from her sobs.

Finally, she calms down and the sniffling dies down. I slowly release her and we both let out a deep sigh at the same time, then we laugh.

"Well, that was just plain beautiful," Caleb says, pretending to wipe a tear from the corner of his eye.

"Oh, shut up." I turn back to Jimi and I think this is the first time she's flashed me a genuine smile since I arrived eight days ago. "Want to help me do something?"

She nods. "You name it."

I let out another sigh and glance over my shoulder at Caleb before I continue. "I need to figure out how I'm going to break it to my parents that I'm not majoring in business this fall. I'm changing my major to music."

"No sweat, but first we have to figure out how we're going to break it to *our* parents that you and Caleb will be sharing a room for the rest of the summer."

CHAPTER TWENTY-EIGHT

THERE IS NO BIRTHDAY gift I could give Claire that would ever compare to having all our children under the same roof, and getting along, for the first time in eighteen years. And we may have missed all of Abby's birthdays, but I know that we will do anything not to miss another for the rest of our lives.

She's back. Abby came back to us, just the way we always hoped she would.

In the first years of our marriage, Claire and I were very open with each other about how it felt to lose Abby. But as the years went by, and the topic was broached less often, it became more unsettling. For the last few years, as we anticipated her eighteenth birthday, it was almost taboo to bring up the subject of Abby.

I anticipated the sadness I'd feel over losing her again, if she decided not to meet us. And the anger I might feel toward Claire when all those feelings of loss were dredged up again. But I never expected to get Abby back only to have to push her away.

So, as I watch Claire as she watches Abby taking a nap with Ryder, I truly know how Claire feels. I don't want my baby girl to ever go away. But, as painful as it is to admit, I have to accept that she was Brian and Lynette's baby girl first.

"Why can't she stay? Look at them." She watches them with a mixture of longing and anger. "It's not fair. It wasn't fair then and it's not fair now."

"Babe, do I need to give you the same life-isn't-fair speech I give the kids?"

"Please spare me." She turns to me and wraps her arms around my waist as she buries her face in my neck. "Please don't make her go."

I hold her tightly and kiss the top of her head. "I can't speak for you, but this has been the best seven weeks of my life. But I've been living in a fool's paradise. This was always going to end. You know that as well as I do."

CASSIA LEO

"But I don't feel right keeping this from Abby. She should know her parents are coming tomorrow."

I thought my reaction to Abby and Caleb sharing a room was extreme. When I came home from Carolina Beach six weeks ago to find Jimi and Abby sitting next to each other on the sofa in the living room, watching videos on Abby's phone, I almost cried tears of joy. It was the most beautiful thing I've ever seen in my life. But they shrugged off my excitement, as if it was no big deal, like it was inevitable that they would become the best of friends. But when they explained the new sleeping arrangements to me, I could feel my eye twitching.

Luckily, Claire pulled me aside before I had the chance to accuse Caleb of orchestrating this new friendship between Jimi and Abby so he could sleep with my daughter. Claire talked some sense into me and promised she would have a discussion with them about... protection. Just the thought of it makes me want to bash Caleb in the head with my '68 Stratocaster. See how cool he thinks it is then.

But after six weeks with the new sleeping arrangements and six weeks of family dinners without any sniping between Jimi and Abby, I'll admit Caleb has worked his way back into my good graces. In fact,

Claire and Abby may never hear me say this aloud, but I'm actually very grateful for him. He takes care of my girl better than I ever could.

So I'm very disappointed with Lynette and Brian's reaction. I wasn't aware that Abby had been lying to her parents about the sleeping arrangements. Then they called Claire last night to accuse us of giving Abby the "bright idea" of changing her major from business to music. Claire was obviously confused and upset that they were accusing us of doing something so underhanded.

I grabbed the phone out of Claire's hand. "What's going on here?"

There was a shuffling on the other end, then Brian came on. "Did you tell my daughter it would be a good idea for her to major in music? Do you get your kicks off of ruining our lives? Now you have to try to ruin Abby's?"

"First of all, I had no idea Abby was changing her major. This is the first I've heard of this. And second of all, I'm not the one ruining Abby's life. If she wants to change her major to music, it's obviously because that's what she wants to do with her life. You should support her decision instead of calling me and my wife to accuse us of meddling in her academic career."

"All you've done this summer is meddle in our lives! If I had any legal recourse, I'd have had Abby forcefully removed from your home weeks ago. She's probably playing music, smoking dope, and having unprotected sex, like her wonderful parents."

"Are you fucking serious? From what I can tell, Abby is happier here with her siblings and her freedom than she has ever been. And if she's thinking of changing her major, it's only because she's trying to stay true to herself. And if you had any sense at all, you'd see how fucking talented she is and how changing her major is a good thing. And, as for unprotected sex, she can do that anywhere. She doesn't need to share a room or an apartment with her boyfriend to do that."

"Is she sharing a room with Caleb?"

I could have lied, but I was so pissed off at Brian's delusional ranting, I didn't think he could take it one step further and threaten to come get her himself. I want to tell Abby that her parents are coming for her tomorrow, but that would probably send her and Caleb off somewhere, to a motel or somewhere worse, just so she could avoid dealing with them. But if I don't tell her, and she finds out I knew, it will be as if I condone Lynette and Brian's attempt to corner her.

I keep hoping that once they see Abby and hear her side, they'll understand how much she loves music. I'll offer to get her a vocal coach and start laying down some tracks in the studio. With my help, Abby can be extremely successful. Since starting my own label thirteen years ago, I've helped launch the careers of more than thirty bands and eight solo artists. Nothing would make me happier than to help my daughter achieve her dreams.

I take Claire's face in my hands and kiss her forehead. "It's going to work out. I promise. But you have to promise me that you're not going to encourage Abby to distance herself even further from Lynette and Brian. You have to remind her how important it is that she has them in her life, even if they don't approve of her career choices or her choice of roommate. Promise me you'll do that? For Abby?"

She lets out a heavy sigh and nods. "Fine. But if they try to push her to do something she doesn't want to do, they're the only ones who can be blamed for alienating her. If I want to offer her comfort or a place to stay when they push her away, you can't fault me for that."

I kiss the corner of her mouth then turn her around so we can both watch Abby and Ryder as they nap on Jimi's bed. At first it worried me when I found Abby taking a nap. But Caleb assured me that it's common for her. It's only natural that Ryder, my little night owl and Abby's biggest admirer, would eventually work his way into the bed with Abby for the most adorable nap time ever.

"Can you imagine what it would be like to see Abby performing for a crowd of ten thousand screaming fans?"

Claire chuckles. "Don't get ahead of yourself. You still have to see if that's what she's interested in."

"I've only known her for eight weeks, but I can honestly say it's what she was born to do. We just have to convince the Jensens that Abby knows herself better than they do."

PART THREE:

Abby

"My heart danced its final dance...
as if nobody was watching."

CHAPTER TWENTY-NINE

Abby

CALEB WAS NOT too thrilled about the prospect of going shopping with Jimi and me. But when I told him it was August 9th, Claire's birthday, he decided he would brave the experience so he could get her a gift.

Caleb was lucky that his boss at the tire shop needed to give his teenage son a job for the summer. It worked out great for both him and Caleb, so he agreed to let Caleb take the summer off to come with me to the beach house. Of course, without the extra income, we needed to work something out with Caleb's roommate, Greg. And Caleb was very grateful that Chris and Claire offered to pay his half of the rent while he's been staying with us at the beach house.

So Caleb was actually happy for the opportunity to go shopping with Jimi and me today. He's been wanting to get something for Claire that would show his appreciation before we leave on Tuesday.

"Do you think she'll like these?" Caleb asks, holding up a pair of four-inch-long turquoise earrings over his earlobes.

"I don't know if she'll like them, but I sure do." I growl at him and he shakes his head to make the earrings wiggle.

He sets the earrings back into a basket of accessories on the counter in The Blue Fedora and we continue toward the gray velvet sofa where Jimi is talking to Chris on my phone.

"Why do we have to be back so soon? Dinner isn't until seven."

She rolls her eyes as Chris speaks. Though we can't hear what he's saying, I'm sure he's given her a perfectly acceptable reason. Finally, she ends the call and hands me the phone.

"He said we have to be back in forty-five minutes."

"But we just got here," I reply, tucking the phone in my purse.

"Yeah, but he said he has his reasons and not to question him. Ugh. He's probably planning some kind of surprise for my mom or something."

I sit down on the sofa next to her. "Well, you know your mom better than any of us. What do you think she'd want?"

"*Our* mom."

"Right. Still getting used to it."

"Honestly, she hates this store. But there's a used bookstore just a few miles north of here that she goes to sometimes. That's where she got a lot of the books in the library. Maybe we can find something there."

"Let's go."

It takes a little less than ten minutes for us to make it to The Bookery on Market Street, but there's no parking. Caleb agrees to drop us off in front of the shop and he sets off down the street to look for a space. The frantic short drive across town combined with the sticky August humidity has me feeling a bit woozy and overheated. When we enter the cool interior of The Bookery, I grab the edge of a wooden table and draw in a long breath.

The sweet smell of old books is intoxicating. It transports us to another time and I instantly know that this is the right place. This is where we'll find the perfect gift.

Jimi stops at the mouth of a long aisle of books

and glances at me over her shoulder. "Are you coming?"

I nod as I let go of the wooden table and set off behind her. The aisle we're in is designated for 19th-century classics. I don't know which of these books Claire has liked or read, but it seems like a good place to start.

"Have you read this?" Jimi asks, holding up a copy of *Jane Eyre.*

"Yeah, we read that last year. I don't read much, but it's one of my favorite books. Does your mom—" Jimi raises an eyebrow. "Does *our* mom like *Jane Eyre?*"

"She has at least two copies of it. It's one of her favorites," she says, putting the book back on the shelf. "Why is it so hard for you to call her Mom? I haven't heard you call them Mom or Dad the whole time you've been here."

I swallow hard as my heart begins to race. This isn't the kind of conversation I expected to have while perusing the shelves.

"I don't know. I guess… I guess I just wonder if it would sound weird. You don't think that would be weird? I've only known them for a few weeks."

She shrugs as she grabs a worn paperback copy of *Great Expectations* off the shelf. "I don't know how these things work. But it seems more weird to me that you don't call them anything at all. Like, what do you call them inside your head? Chris and Claire?" She laughs at this suggestion as if it's ludicrous and I feel the heat rising in my cheeks. Her eyes widen when she sees my reaction. "I'm sorry. I didn't mean that the way it sounded. I mean, of course that's probably how you think of them. *Shit*. I feel like an idiot. Just forget I said anything."

I gently take the book from her and turn it over in my hands a couple of times. "Does she have this one?" I ask, viscerally aware that I just referred to Claire as *she*. And now I just referred to her in my head as *Claire*.

"I don't think so. I haven't seen it in the library. Have you?"

I chuckle at the awkward tone in her voice. "You're right. After everything they've done for me, and for Caleb, I should at least try to break that large wall of ice standing between us."

"Hey, don't do it on my account."

"Don't do what on your account?" Caleb asks as he enters the aisle, his face flushed pink from the heat.

Jimi glances at me as if to say, "This is all yours."

"Nothing. I just… I think I want to go back. I want to go home."

"But we didn't get anything."

Jimi smiles as she squeezes past us to leave the aisle. I look up at Caleb and he's confused. "We can't find anything here that she can't get on her own. Let's go."

His shoulders slump with frustration. "Fine. Just wait in here while I go get the car. It's hotter than Satan's ass crack out there."

We make one stop at a local bakery to pick up the birthday cake Jimi ordered, then we pull into the driveway a few minutes before the forty-five-minute deadline. Caleb carries the cake into the kitchen and Jimi helps him make room for it in the refrigerator while I look for Claire. I'm not surprised to find her upstairs in the laundry room, working on her birthday. She slams the dryer shut and when she spins around to leave, she jumps at the sight of me.

"Oh, my God. You scared me," she says, clutching her chest. "Do you have something you need washed?" I shake my head and she looks confused. "Are you okay? Are you out of medicine? What's wrong?"

I shake my head again. "Nothing's wrong. In fact, everything couldn't be more right. And I have you to thank for that. So I just want to say… Thank you… for everything you've done for Caleb and me. And…

Happy birthday… Mom."

Her whole body trembles as she reaches up to cover her mouth. "Oh, God," she whispers.

Her chest is heaving so hard and her hands are shaking uncontrollably. It actually scares me.

I lightly place my hand on her shoulder. "Are you okay?"

She nods furiously, but she still can't speak, so I do the one thing I hope will help. I slowly wrap my arms around her waist and she lets out a soft cry as she takes me in her arms.

"Oh, Abby," she whispers. "I have never heard anything so beautiful in all my life."

We hold each other a moment longer until she's no longer trembling. When she releases me, Jimi comes bounding up the stairs. She looks a bit surprised when she sees us both standing just inside the laundry room, crying. Then she smiles as she realizes her little pep talk at the used bookstore worked.

But her smile disappears quickly. "Someone's here."

"Who?" I ask, but Jimi doesn't answer. She casts us an ominous look as she turns around and heads back down the steps.

I turn to Claire and she's wringing her hands as she

looks me in the eye. "Your... your parents are here to take you home."

My chest aches with the force of my heart pounding. I race down the steps and I can't believe what I'm seeing. My mom and dad are standing in the living room. My dad's arms are crossed over his bulky chest and my mom's lips are pressed together in a hard line across her face.

My dad speaks first. "Get your things. We're going home."

"I'm not leaving right now. I'm leaving with Caleb on Tuesday."

My mom rolls her eyes as she steps forward. "Just get your things and get in the car, Abby. We've allowed you to live your little hard-rock fantasy long enough. It's time to go home and get ready for school."

"Hard-rock fantasy? Are you kidding me? This has been the best summer of my life and you're calling it a fantasy?"

"Oh, please, Abby. Of course it's the best summer of your life. And who knows how much damage you've done to your heart in the meantime?"

Caleb comes up behind me and places his hands on my shoulders and my dad casts a vicious glare in his direction. "Abby has been doing great," Caleb says, squeezing my arm. "She's been taking all her meds and I think the physical activity has been helping. She has less—"

"Physical *activity*?" My dad cuts him off. "Are you two having *sex*?"

"Don't answer that!" I shout at Caleb, then I round on my dad. "It's none of your business what Caleb and I do, just like it's none of *my* business what you and Mom do in the bedroom. I'm an adult and I'm not stupid. A little trust wouldn't hurt, Dad. I've never given you a reason not to trust me."

Chris and Claire come down the stairs and I must admit that I'm happy to see the angry look on Chris's face. Then I remember how Claire already knew my parents were coming, which means Chris probably knew, as well.

"Did you know they were coming?"

Chris nods his head. "I'm sorry, Abby. We wanted to tell you, but they asked us not to. And we really didn't want to cause any more trouble for you all. It's really hard being in the middle of this. We really just want whatever makes you happy."

My mom laughs at this. "Of course. Take the path of least resistance so we're the bad guys. You were right, Brian. You knew this would happen."

"Lynette, I think there's been a grave misunderstanding here," Chris continues. "We've done everything you asked of us seventeen and a half years ago. We stayed away. We didn't tie you guys up in an expensive legal battle. We did it all for Abby's sake. Which is why I have to set my foot down here. I truly believe what you're doing is not in her best interests. I think it's time for you all to step aside and let Abby make some decisions for herself. She's an adult and a very intelligent soul. She deserves for all of us to put some faith in her."

My mom shakes her head. "You don't know the first thing about my daughter. You've spent eight weeks with her. I've spent eighteen years with her." She grabs my hand and I yank it back. "Don't be difficult, Abby. Just come home and we can get your stuff later."

I look around the room and realize that Ryder and Junior have joined Jimi. They're all three standing in the hallway and my stomach drops when I see Ryder crying. Caleb lets go of my shoulders as I walk toward them. Ryder leans against the wall, his face turned toward the wallpaper to hide his tears.

I lean down and whisper in his ear, "I'm not going anywhere."

Then I turn to Jimi and look her in the eye as I mouth the word "keys." She slowly slides her hand into the pocket of her shorts and discreetly hands me the key to her Mercedes. Junior smiles when he sees this exchange.

I slip the key into my pocket, then I turn on my heel and head right past my parents toward the back door.

"Where are you going?" my mom calls out to me.

I keep going, my feet flying down the back steps. I pull the keys out of my pocket and hit the button on the key fob to deactivate the alarm.

"Abby, come back here!" she shrieks as I slide into the driver's seat of Jimi's black Mercedes.

My hand is shaking as I jam the key into the ignition. The smell of leather is making me even more nervous. I've never driven a car this expensive. Actually, I've hardly driven any car of any value. I'm not sure I can safely drive Jimi's Mercedes. If I crash today, I guess I can thank my fabulous parents and their need to protect my fragile heart.

I turn the key and the engine hums. I shift into reverse and punch the gas pedal, then I nearly pass out when the car jumps backward into the driveway, almost crashing into the block wall separating the beach house from the neighbor's house. My mom comes bounding out of the front door. I quickly switch gears and peel out of the driveway onto Sandpiper Street, then I head toward Lumina Avenue.

I don't know if anyone will follow me. I hope they don't. I just need to get away.

For eighteen years, I was the sickly, fragile daughter of Brian and Lynette Jensen. Now… I don't know who I am. When I'm with my biological parents, I don't feel like the frail girl I was eight weeks ago. I'm different. I'm the girl who got away. The girl who was strong enough to capture my parents' hearts in a single twenty-minute meeting and hold them captive for eighteen years.

That's the girl I want to be. I don't want to be fragile anymore.

I turn left on Lumina and the Mercedes grips the slick asphalt beautifully. Racing forward, I turn right onto Highway 74 and draw in a deep breath. I don't know where I'm going. All I know is that I can't be there right now. I need to think without my mom's pitiful gaze penetrating me. Or the look of disappointment and hope in Chris and Claire's eyes.

I touch the power button on the touchscreen and Jimi's favorite playlist begins to play. I listen to the beachy, acoustic melodies and think of the past few weeks. Flashes of my parents' hopeful faces flicker in my mind. Caleb's face materializes, and memories of that day on the beach come rushing back to me. My body relaxes and my hands stop trembling as a smile curls my lips. Caleb is my constant.

Even when I'm being pulled this way and that way, it's Caleb's face, his sturdy hands, his breath so soft on my skin, his love so fragile in my hands… Caleb is the rope that keeps me tethered to reality. As long as I have Caleb, I'll get through this.

A buzzing noise pulls me out of my thoughts and I glance at the cup holder between the seats. My phone is flashing. I pick it up and glance at the screen. It's Caleb.

I heave a deep sigh and answer. "Hello?"

When I turn my attention back to the road, something is wrong. The lane has moved. Or… Oh, no. It's not the lane. It's my car that's veered into oncoming traffic. The last thing I hear is Caleb screaming my name before I drop the phone.

CHAPTER THIRTY

Caleb

I SMILE AS I WATCH her get into Jimi's Mercedes. My sunshine has balls. Then my smile disappears as I remember how little driving experience she has. I shouldn't be standing here with a smile on my face. I should be chasing Abby.

"I'll get her!" I shout, blowing past Lynette and Brian who are standing in the middle of the driveway, dumbfounded.

I hop into the 'Cuda, silently thanking myself for leaving the top down. I blast the car horn for them to move out of my way so I can pull out of the driveway. It takes them a couple of seconds to figure out what's going on. A couple of the longest seconds of my life. I want to shout at them to get out of the fucking way. Finally, I pull the 'Cuda out of the driveway and peel out down the street.

She's not even on Sandpiper anymore. She must have turned left or right on Lumina already, but I have no idea which way she went. I make it to the end of the street and inch forward into oncoming traffic, trying to get a glimpse of Jimi's Mercedes speeding away in either direction. A horn blares in my left ear as the 'Cuda's nose juts out into the street. I don't give a shit. I'd block all the traffic on this damn street if that's what it takes to find Abby.

Then I see it! The black Mercedes is heading for the Highway 74 on-ramp. I pound the horn a few times to warn people as I punch the gas pedal and gun it onto Lumina. I swerve to avoid a woman who's getting ready to jaywalk, then I maneuver around a slow-moving pickup truck and spit curses when I hit a red light.

"Fuck!"

A large crowd of pedestrians crosses Lumina toward the beach, completely oblivious to the fact that their need to get to the water could cost Abby her life. I want to shout at them to hurry the fuck up. Instead, I tap the steering wheel anxiously. Once the pedestrians have passed, I inch forward, checking for cross-traffic. A single gold Buick crosses Lumina, then I punch the gas, running the red light and leaving the car horns and slow pedestrians behind me.

My tires squeal as I turn onto Highway 74 at a dangerous speed. The 'Cuda fishtails a little on the on-ramp, but I manage to get it back under my control and I race forward onto the highway. I need to call her and tell her to pull over.

I fish my phone out of my pocket, glancing back and forth between the screen and the road as I hold down the voice command button and tell my phone to call Abby.

"Calling Gabby," the pleasant voice responds.

"No!" I shout at the phone. "Call Sunshine! Call Sunshine!"

Fuck. Why did I have to change her name in my phone?

"Calling Sunshine," the voice says and I let out a sigh of frustration.

The car in front of me slows down to exit, so I begin to switch lanes to get around them and the car next to me blares their horn.

"Shit!"

I try to swerve back into my lane, but the car in

front of me has slowed down so much I'm going to clip his rear bumper.

"Hello?" Abby's voice is soft, almost tired, and it's the last thing I hear before I drop the phone onto the floor of the passenger side.

I slam on the brakes to avoid hitting the car in front of me, grumbling as I wait for the car to exit the highway. Then I punch the gas again for two reasons. First, so I can catch up with Abby. And second, so the inertia will make the phone slide backward across the floor of the car toward me.

I keep one eye on the road in front of me as I reach for the phone, but it's just out of my reach. I take one long look at the road ahead of me and it's clear, so I take a chance. Keeping one hand on the steering wheel, I throw myself across the seat and grab the phone.

"Abby!"

When I sit up, the 'Cuda is drifting to the left, right into an eighteen-wheeler truck. I swerve to the right, but I overcorrect and my 65-year-old car shreds through the guard railing as if it were Swiss cheese. The front wheel goes over the edge of the overpass and my first instinct is to slam on the brakes. But the moment I do this, the tail of the 'Cuda flies upward as the nose goes over the edge. All I can think as I'm thrown from the car into the deep ravine is that I failed.

CHAPTER THIRTY-ONE

Abby

I SWERVE to bring my car back into the right lane, but the damage is done. My heart is pounding so hard and fast I can't breathe. A sharp pain slices through my left shoulder and I double over the steering wheel. I press my foot down on the brake, but my right arm doesn't respond when I try to reach for the gearshift. I throw my left arm across my body and push the gearshift into park. The cacophony of horns blaring around me is barely audible as I slump over the center console and black out.

Claire

I KNOW CHRIS IS driving as fast as he can, well over the speed limit, without putting us in danger. But I just want to tell him to hurry up. The sound of Jimi's sobs coming from the backseat are only making this worse.

"I'm sorry," she declares through her tears. "I'm sorry I gave her the keys."

I reach back and squeeze her knee. "It's not your fault."

"Yes, it is." She pushes my hand away and pulls her feet up onto the seat to hug her knees. "I shouldn't even go. I don't deserve to be there."

"Don't say that," Ryder says, his voice gruff from crying. He presses his fist into his forehead, as he shakes his head. "Nothing is wrong with Abby. Tell her, Mom. Tell her Abby's fine."

I don't know how to respond, so I turn to Junior, but he's just staring out the car window. He never makes a sound and his eyes never blink. We tried calling Caleb, but he never answered. Then, shortly after Brian received the call that Abby was at New Hanover Regional Medical Center, Lynette received another call as we were loading into our separate vehicles to head to the hospital. Caleb was also in the hospital. They wouldn't give us Caleb's status over the phone, but they told us that Abby was in surgery after suffering a heart attack and a stroke.

They actually told us she was lucky that she was able to stop the car and get into park before she passed out. I want to believe she's lucky, but it's hard to see it that way when she's currently undergoing a surgery that can either save her or kill her. And *if* she wakes up, I have no idea if she'll have Caleb there to comfort her.

"Abby's going to be fine, baby," I assure Ryder. "Everything's going to be fine."

I turn forward so the kids can't see how much I don't believe the words I just spoke. I can't even bring myself to look at Chris. I don't want to know how this is surely tearing him apart.

Chris drops me off near the emergency-room entrance, then he sets off with the kids to find a parking space. I race inside and dart toward the reception area. I don't think the Jensens are here yet.

"Excuse me, miss. I'm here for Abigail Jensen."

The woman behind the plexiglass divider has frizzy auburn hair pinned back in a silver barrette. She looks up at me from her computer keyboard with a bored expression. "Is she a patient?"

"Yes, she's a patient! She was just brought in here with a heart attack and stroke. She's... she's eighteen."

She nods as she recognizes who I'm talking about. "Oh, yeah. She's in surgery. Are you the mother? I need you to sign some paperwork."

I cover my mouth as I blink back tears and try not to answer this question the way I want to.

She looks stricken by my sudden gust of emotion. "I'm sorry, ma'am. If you need a moment to compose yourself, we can leave the paperwork for later."

"No, it's fine. I'm... I'm not her mother. Well, not legally. I'm her biological mother. Her adoptive mother should be here soon. Oh, God. Please just tell me she's okay."

"I'm sorry, ma'am, but we don't have any news. You're going to have to wait until she's out of surgery. I'm sure Dr. Givens will debrief you as soon as she's stabilized."

I turn around and Ryder races toward me. "Where is she?"

"She's in surgery, sweetheart. We have to wait."

Chris, Junior, and Jimi follow after him and we all walk solemnly toward the other side of the beige and blue waiting room. The Jensens arrive a few minutes later and they get the same spiel from the woman behind the glass, but Lynette bravely sits down with her to fill out the paperwork. And, as I watch her filling out the forms while periodically wiping away her tears, for the first time in my life, I wish I could help her. I wish I could fill out the damn forms about Abby's medical history and insurance information. I wish I knew a damn thing about any of that stuff.

Six hours and forty minutes later, Dr. Givens enters the waiting room and we all rise from our chairs to flock to him. His brown skin shimmers in the fluorescent lighting, but it doesn't hide how tired he is. He lets out a soft sigh before he begins.

"As you know, Abigail suffered a severe heart attack, which dislodged a tiny blood clot that most likely originated in her heart. The clot traveled into the outer branch of the middle cerebral artery in her brain, causing a minor stroke. We believe that she didn't sustain any cognitive damage. But it turns out the heart attack was much worse than we anticipated."

"How much worse?" Lynette asks.

Dr. Givens pauses for a moment then lets out

another sigh. "The trauma of the accident caused Abby to go into circulatory collapse. She was very lucky that she was only six minutes away from the hospital. We were able to get her heart started again and we put a temporary stent in two of her arteries to keep them from collapsing again. However, both the collapse and the stroke have caused too much stress on her heart. She's on a respirator and in a medically induced coma right now… She won't survive much longer without a new heart."

"Then get her a new heart!" Chris roars. "I'll pay for it. I'll fly it here if I have to. Just make it happen!"

"That won't be necessary."

"What do you mean? You can't let her die!" Lynette shrieks.

"No, what I mean is that we already have a heart. Here in this hospital."

Chris shakes his head. "That fast? Then, what are you waiting for?"

"Well, it's a bit complicated. The eighteen-year-old male who was brought in at the same time as Abby… he had this in his wallet."

Givens holds out a white plastic card. The front of the card reads "Living will in place for Caleb Everett. In the event of an emergency, please contact Gill

Burrows."

"We contacted Mr. Burrows and it turns out he's the lawyer who drafted Caleb's living will. Mr. Everett's wishes were for Abigail to have his heart."

My knees give out and I grasp the arm of the chair next to me to keep from collapsing. Chris and the doctor kneel next to me, repeatedly asking if I'm okay.

I shake my head. "This will destroy her."

Givens orders Jimi to get me some water from the cooler in the corner of the waiting room, then he stands up so he can address everyone. "We have a legal obligation to carry out Mr. Everett's wishes. In the event that he were permanently incapacitated, he wanted Abigail to have his heart. Since Abigail is an adult and she doesn't have a living will in place, we have a legal and moral obligation to preserve her life to the best of our ability. This is her best chance."

I climb onto the chair to have a seat and sip the water that Jimi brought for me. I can't bring myself to speak. I couldn't imagine living without Chris and I know Abby will be devastated when she wakes up to find that Caleb didn't make it. I can only hope that having a part of Caleb inside her will make it easier, but somehow I seriously doubt that.

Chris stands up and I watch as he and Brian

exchange a silent agreement. Then Brian turns to Dr. Givens and nods. "Do it. Save my little girl."

CHAPTER THIRTY-TWO

THIS IS THE FOURTH time I've opened my eyes in this hospital room. The tube in my throat is finally gone. I have vague memories of my parents standing at my bedside, wearing gloves and masks. I think I remember being wheeled into an X-ray room. I'm so thirsty.

"Mom?"

A nurse in purple scrubs and a mint-green mask over her mouth arrives at my bedside. "How are you feeling, sweetie?"

There are less machines beeping than there were the last time I woke up. My entire body feels sore, as if I did a hundred dead lifts recently. But the soreness in my chest is the worst. I've obviously undergone another heart surgery. I remember this pain.

"Where are my parents?"

"They went back to the hotel to change their clothes. They should be back in just a few minutes. Your… your *other* parents are outside. Can I send them in?"

"Where's Caleb?" My voice cracks on Caleb's name. "Why is it so cold in here?"

"You're running a slight fever. You're on a high dose of anti-rejection meds right now, and that suppresses your immune system."

"Anti-rejection?"

The nurse finishes checking the drainage tubes coming out of my chest. "I'll let your family explain everything."

She leaves the room and I feel so alone. This room is so cold. It's not a regular hospital recovery room. It looks cold and lifeless like a surgical room. And there's a small antechamber off to my left where the nurse removes her gloves and mask before she tosses them into a waste bin. She steps out into the corridor for a moment, then she comes back into the antechamber with Chris and Claire. They spend at least five minutes scrubbing their hands and arms, then all three of them put on more gloves and masks.

As they approach my bed, something feels different. Quiet. Too quiet.

"How long have I been here?"

Claire's eyes are puffy and glistening. "Fifty-two hours."

"More than two days? Where's Caleb?"

Claire opens her mouth to say something, then she stops herself and turns away.

Chris looks me in the eye and flashes me a weak smile. "Your parents will talk to you about Caleb."

"Why? Where is he?"

Claire turns around and leaves the room without another word and Chris looks stumped.

"Please tell me what's going on here. I wake up with tubes coming out of every hole in my body and the nurse just said something to me about anti-rejection meds. Did I get a heart transplant? What happened? Please... I'm scared."

Chris hangs his head for a moment and when he lifts it again, there are tears in his eyes. "I don't want to be the one to break your heart. Please don't make me do this."

The heart-rate monitor starts beeping loudly as my pulse races. The nurse is at my side a second later, injecting something into my IV line. Within seconds, drowsiness overtakes me and I drift off with Caleb's name on my lips.

THE FIFTH TIME I wake, my parents are there. My dad is standing like a soldier at my bedside, his hands behind his back, his chin dimpled with the effort of holding back his emotions. My mom stands right next to him, her gloved hand wrapped tightly around my fingers.

"Don't lie to me," I whisper through the tears.

"I won't lie to you, sweetheart," my dad says, his voice thick with emotion. "But I think Caleb would rather tell you everything himself."

I open my mouth to curse him for lying to me by pretending that Caleb is alive, but before I can speak another word, he pulls a white envelope from behind his back. The sight of my name on the outside of the envelope in Caleb's messy scrawl sends a bolt of pain through my chest.

"I wanted to wait to give you this later, but I don't think Caleb would have wanted that."

"Stop talking about him like… that."

I want to tell my dad to stop talking about Caleb like he's gone, but I can't bring myself to say the words. I draw in a long breath as I take the envelope from my dad's large hand.

"We haven't read it. We just opened it to make it easier for you," he assures me as he takes a step back.

"We'll be right outside, honey." My mom squeezes the words out through her tears.

I hold the envelope up in front of my face and stare at the letters A-B-B-Y and I imagine Caleb sitting at the table in the apartment he shared with Greg. I imagine his beautiful fingers curled around the pen as it slid across the paper. When did he write me this letter? What was he thinking?

I guess I'm about to find out.

I lay the envelope on my belly, then I struggle a bit to slip the folded piece of white paper out with just one hand. But a few seconds later, I have the paper out of the envelope and unfolded. I lay it facedown on my belly for a moment.

Caleb, wherever you are, please give me the strength to make it through this.

I sniff loudly and let out a long sigh. Then I lift the paper off my stomach and read.

Abby,

How do you thank someone for giving you a reason to live? I've thought about this a lot over the last few years since you came into my life. And for three years, I came up with nothing.

Then my dad died and there you were again. My friend. My girl. My sunshine, bringing light to my darkest days.

When the estate lawyer called me to his office to pick up the inheritance check in January after my eighteenth birthday, it got me thinking about what I wanted to leave behind after my death. Like my dad, I don't have much to give, but I do have one thing I hope will still be useful when I go. Something you fixed up and made all shiny and new for me.

My heart.

Abby, the first time I spoke to you in the hospital, my heart danced. And I don't think it ever stopped. You gave my heart quite a workout, sunshine. So I know that the moment they took my heart out of my chest and put it in yours, my heart danced its final dance as if nobody was watching.

You can be anything you want to be now. Chase your dreams, Abby.

Always yours,
Caleb

I throw the letter over the edge of the bed and try

to breathe, but I'm in so much pain, breathing seems secondary. The nurse rushes in and injects something into my IV line again.

I open my mouth to speak, but nothing comes out except for a soft squeak.

"What did you say, sweetie?"

The drowsiness is taking hold again, and my throat relaxes enough for me to get out four words. "You *were* my dream."

CHAPTER THIRTY-THREE

I SPEND SEVENTEEN excruciating days in the hospital, unable to speak or eat. It's only my desire to see the endless biopsies and X-rays end that makes me take up solid food again. I need it all to be over. I need to go home, curl up in my bed, and sleep for a very long time. My dreams are the only place where I'm safe. My dreams are the only place where none of this ever happened.

The ride home from the hospital is the longest three hours of my life. The ride should have taken two and a half hours, but my dad insists on driving below the speed limit. Afraid my new heart might fall out or something. My mom is sitting in the backseat with me, wringing her hands with frustration because I won't allow her to touch me.

I don't want my mother to hold me while I sob on her shoulder and ask, "Why me?" I want Caleb to hold me and tell me I'm going to get through this. That losing him isn't the end of every good thing in my life.

I just want to hear his voice one more time. Is that too much to ask? I think it would be easier if I could just hear him call me "sunshine" once more.

We enter our house in Raleigh and the first thing I'm struck by is the smell. The beach house always had a slightly salty, sunbaked aroma mixed with the scent of fresh laundry. With seven people in the house, there was always a load going. Our house in Raleigh smells like my mom's favorite lemon-scented disinfectant. She must have disinfected every surface with that stuff when she and my dad came home a few days ago to prepare the house for my arrival.

I want to take a shower, but I'm not allowed to for another twelve days. And my mom is supposed to help me when I take a bath, so that rules out that option. I head for the kitchen to get myself a glass of water and my mom follows close behind me.

"Are you hungry, honey? I got a bunch of healthy snacks that are on the list Dr. Rosenthal gave me. We have tons of fruits and veggies, low-fat cheese sticks, gluten-free rice crackers."

"I'm not hungry. I just want a glass of water." I reach for the cupboard above the kitchen counter, but a sharp pain in my breastbone stops me.

"I'll get you some water. You just go lie down."

She grabs my arms and gently turns me away from the counter. I take a couple of steps forward, then I stop in the middle of the kitchen and look around. The beige stone tiles and cherry cabinets look the same as they did when I was last here, but something about this room is different.

"What did you change in here?"

My mom glances toward the kitchen window above the sink. "We removed all the blinds and curtains in the house."

"In my room, too?"

"No." She swiftly grabs a glass from the cupboard and fills it with water, then she places her hand on the small of my back to lead me to my bedroom. "Chris and Claire helped us install some remote-controlled window coverings in your room. The remote is in the top drawer of your nightstand. I know you probably don't feel like it, but please consider leaving the blinds open as often as possible. It's better for you. You

know the saying. Sunlight is the best disinfectant. Turns out that's also true in the literal sense."

I stand on the threshold of my bedroom and marvel at how clean and organized everything is. The dozens of pictures of me, Caleb, and Amy that were pinned haphazardly on the walls are now arranged in a beautiful collage in a single picture frame that hangs above my headboard. The messy collection of office supplies and makeup on my desk is gone and a handy purple makeup case sits next to my laptop. Both my guitars hang from hooks on the wall. The room smells like lemon instead of the usual combined scent of shampoo and dirty socks. Everything has been organized and sanitized, except for the full-length mirror propped up against the wall in the corner. Where Caleb wrote with a tube of cherry lip balm, "Good morning, sunshine!"

I step inside the room and grab the handle of the door. "I'm going to sleep."

"Don't forget your water."

I take the glass from her and quickly close the door before she can give me any sage advice about how to get over Caleb. I set the glass of water on the nightstand, then I open the top drawer and easily find the small white remote for the window coverings. I scoop it up and press the down arrow button until the blinds and the new ivory curtains are completely closed.

I switch on my bedside lamp and stare at the mirror in the corner for a while before I gather the courage to sit down at my desk. Opening the laptop, my heart jumps when I see the desktop background. It's a picture of Caleb and me in the quad at school. His friend Ewan took this picture of us on Caleb's eighteenth birthday in January. I stare at him for a few minutes, searching his face for some sign of what he was planning to do. But I see nothing.

Caleb was always terrible at keeping secrets. Maybe he didn't consider his living will a secret. Maybe he thought of it more as a gift, like the guitar he gave me for my birthday almost five months ago. And since he knew he wouldn't be around to give it to me, he just put it out of his mind.

Well, he had it in his mind long enough to sign the papers and write me a letter. And, according to his estate lawyer, Caleb had one final gift for me. An email he wanted me to read once I was strong enough.

I log into my computer and, for a split second, consider changing the desktop background so I don't have to stare at his smiling face. Or the way his eyebrow got crooked when he smiled hugely. Or the way his hand is pretending to squeeze my breast and I'm laughing so hard you can see my tonsils. If I change this background image, that will be the beginning of forgetting Caleb and, as painful as it is to remember, I think I'd rather die than forget him.

I open up my email program and it takes about five minutes for thousands of emails to load. There are emails from almost every single person in my senior high school class, expressing their condolences for Caleb's death. There are more emails from people I don't know than there are from people whose names I vaguely recognize.

I search my inbox for "Gill Burrows" and quickly find the email I'm looking for. The subject line reads: Caleb's final request. My cursor hovers over the message, just waiting for me to double-click to open it. But I can't. If I open that email, that will be it. I will never hear from him again. I'm not ready to let him go yet.

I minimize the program and close the lid on my laptop. Caleb wanted me to open that message when I was strong enough. And today I'm not. Today, I wonder if I'll ever open that email.

CALEB WAS CREMATED three days after he gave me his heart and his ashes were held in an antique blue and white vase, which had previously graced the shelves in Claire's library. The vase was kept in the library, on the shelf nearest the '68 Stratocaster, until three weeks after his death, three days after I returned home. Then, according to Caleb's instructions, his ashes were to be buried in the ground next to the plot where his father's ashes are buried.

It's a muggy, overcast Labor Day weekend and I've never seen so many people dressed in black gathered in one place. The clouds refuse to part, as if God has shrouded our corner of the earth in a shadow of darkness to pay His respects. I don't want to speak at the memorial. I don't want to bare my heart and soul in front of a crowd of hundreds of mourners. But I can't *not* speak. This isn't just anyone. This is Caleb. This is my heart.

I tread softly over the neatly trimmed grass until I reach the well-worn patch behind the wooden podium where four others have spoken before me. I glance at the crowd and quickly turn back to the speech I have displayed on my phone. The crowd is silent, as this is the moment I'm sure they've all been waiting for.

I draw in a slow breath and let it out, then I begin. "I'm sure Caleb didn't expect such a large turnout or he might have planned something a bit more grandiose." I pause as a few people chuckle and I try to catch my breath. "But that's the way Caleb was, always doing amazingly huge things when no one was looking. He once planned a scavenger hunt for me. It was my sixteenth birthday, so he took me on a tour of our firsts. The first time he saw me in Mr. Wentz's biology classroom. The first time he realized he had a crush on me in Mr. Warner's algebra class. The first time we spoke to each other in my hospital room. And the scavenger hunt ended on my front doorstep, the location of our first kiss. At each location, there was a gift for me and I later found out he had borrowed money from his boss to buy some of those gifts. I should have known then that Caleb would stop at nothing to give me everything."

A surge of raw emotion overcomes me and I stop for a couple of minutes to collect myself. "Caleb wasn't just my boyfriend, he was my caregiver, my study partner, my number-one distraction, my reality check, and my belly laugh when I needed it most. He was the one person who always knew exactly what I needed, exactly when I needed it. So it doesn't surprise me at all that Caleb knew I would need his heart just as much in his death as I needed it when he was alive."

The sobbing in the crowd is almost unbearable. I take a few deep breaths and wipe my face before I continue.

"But if there is anything I think Caleb would most want to be remembered for, I don't think it would be the priceless gift of life he gave to me. I think Caleb would want to be remembered as part of a family, part of your family and mine… So Caleb, wherever you are, thank you for letting me be a part of your family."

I can't escape the podium any faster. The humidity is suffocating and the chest-racking sobs aren't making it any easier to breathe. My dad wraps his arm around my waist and my feet float over the grass as he carries me toward the car. As I collapse into the backseat, I'm surprised to find Ryder sitting back there. He's wearing a handsome dark-gray suit and his eyes are rimmed pink from crying.

"Hey, what are you doing here?"

"I asked your mom and she said it was okay to ride with you. Is that okay?"

"Of course it is."

I stretch my arms out to give him a hug and his nostrils flare as tears spill over his cheeks. He carefully wraps his arms around my waist and we hold each other the whole ride home. By the time my dad pulls the car into the driveway, Chris's Jaguar is already parked on the curb waiting for us.

I kiss Ryder's forehead and slowly let him go. "We're home."

He looks up at me with those brown eyes that stunned me when I first saw them almost three months ago. "Are you coming back? I asked my dad and he said he doesn't know."

"I don't know, Ryder. I'm really behind on my classes right now because of all that time in the hospital. I don't think I can take any more time off. But I'm sure I'll see you soon."

"Maybe you should take the semester off," my mom says, twisting around in the front seat to face me. "All the doctors said these first three to four months are the most critical time. You're going to need a lot of rest. Maybe... Maybe you can spend some of that time with your siblings."

Ryder's eyes light up. I don't want to tell him that I don't know if I'll ever be strong enough to visit him at their house in Cary or the beach house. The place where the best and worst summer of my life began and ended. The place where I got lost in the ocean and found myself in someone else's eyes.

"Come on. Let's go inside."

Ryder looks a little bummed that I didn't provide any input on my mom's suggestion, but he quickly forgets once we're inside the house. My mom serves lemonade and iced tea and we all gather in the living room to reminisce about Caleb. Claire sits in the armchair while Chris and Jimi sit on each arm. My parents and I sit on the sofa while Ryder and Junior sit on the floor next to the coffee table.

"Remember when he let me drive his car?" Junior says, then he takes a sip of his lemonade.

"He did not," Jimi says, shaking her head.

"Yes, he did. He told me not to tell you all 'cause you'd be mad. But he let me drive it down Sandpiper and back to the house. He said he'd never seen a fourteen-year-old drive with such panache. What's panache?"

Chris shakes his head. "Something you definitely do not lack."

Junior's face splits into a wide smile. "Caleb knew me so well."

"How about you, Ryder?" I ask. "What's your

favorite memory of Caleb?"

He shrugs. "The first time we sang in the library?"

"The first time?" Chris asks. "How about the time he taught you to play 'Wild Horses' on your guitar?"

"He never finished teaching me."

For some reason, these words knock the breath out of me. I rise from the sofa and head for my bedroom, where I can grieve in private. I close the door behind me and curl up on my bed, trying to temper the anger building up inside me. The irrational voice in my head telling me I should be angry at Caleb for leaving me.

The knock at the door just annoys me. "I'm fine!"

The door opens a crack. "Abby?"

Claire's voice is unexpected and only makes the tears come faster. "I'm fine, really."

She pushes the door open a little wider so she can stick her head in. "Can I come in?"

I nod, then I sit up and grab a tissue out of the box on my nightstand. She enters and softly closes the door behind her. She has a fat manila envelope in one hand and I imagine it's probably one more thing Caleb left behind that I won't be able to look at.

She sits next to me on the bed and lays the envelope in her lap. "I can't imagine what you must be going through." She reaches across and grabs my hand and the softness of her hand is comforting. "But I was hoping that I could maybe share something with you that might make you feel less alone. You see, when I was very young, my mother homeschooled me. When she was feeling well, which was usually a few hours a day, she would teach me everything she could about reading, math, and science. In our tiny home in the woods, she was my teacher and my classmate, my mother and my friend. We were each other's worlds, so when I lost her at the age of seven, I lost everything. And it took me a very, very long time to recover from that loss. It wasn't until I met your father when I was fifteen that my life began to show any hope of a happy ending."

She opens the manila envelope and removes a large stack of paper from within. She sets the envelope aside and lays the stack of paper on top of her lap.

"After your parents decided that it would be better for us not to be part of your life, I grieved for a while. I hadn't just lost you, I had lost the right to know all the things that would make you who you are today. All the birthdays and holidays. All the school projects and bedtime stories. All the triumphs and failures. All the lessons and heartbreak. I was going to miss all of it.

That was the worst part. But I quickly realized that, if I was diligent, it's possible that you wouldn't have to miss out on any of that stuff."

She hands me the stack of paper and I lay it gently in my lap. "For the past seventeen years, I've kept a journal, an unpublished memoir of sorts. I tried to record all the most important events of our lives over the past seventeen years, in hopes that one day I would be able to gift it to you. And I've documented what I remember most from the time your father and I met up until the day we lost you and beyond. I've tentatively titled this memoir *Shattered Hearts*, but it will never be published. It's for you and only you. I printed you a copy and emailed you the file."

I hug the stack of papers to my chest as I stare at the carpet. "I wish Caleb could read it with me. He... He really loved you guys."

She wraps her arm around my shoulders and squeezes me. "We loved him too. And we love you. It hurts me so much to see you in so much pain." She strokes my hair and I sigh as she wipes the tears from my cheeks. "I just need you to promise me one thing."

"What?"

"Promise me you'll write the last chapter of that book. The one where Abby realizes what a beautiful

CASSIA LEO

second chance at life she's been given and she uses it to get her happily ever after."

I nod and she takes me into her arms, holding me tightly until my body stops trembling. When she finally lets go, I look into her eyes and, for just a brief millisecond, I see her as a seven-year-old girl. If she could survive losing her whole family, like Caleb, then I can survive this. It's time to open that email.

CHAPTER THIRTY-FOUR

Abby

Four months later

I SLIDE INTO THE driver's seat of my new white Volvo and the door closes and locks on its own. I press the start button, then I begin entering the Cary address in the navigation system. I confirm the destination and my self-driving car sets off on the short journey from my house to my *other* house.

I had originally wanted to call them House #1 and House #2, but Junior thought it was so funny that their house was #2. He certainly didn't need any more material for his arsenal. So I settled on "my house" and "my other house."

I mostly stay at my house, but I have spent a couple of weeks at the house in Cary. And I even convinced my parents to spend Christmas with the Knights and the Pollocks. I like to see it as pulling double-duty, making sure Caleb's heart is always surrounded by family.

But today, I'm headed to Cary, in the car Chris insisted he had to buy for me, for a very different reason. It's been four months since I opened Caleb's final email to me. And today would have been Caleb's nineteenth birthday. Today, I'm finally going to fulfill Caleb's final request.

When I opened that email four months ago, I thought my parents were going to have to take me back to the hospital. My heart—Caleb's heart—was pounding so hard just from seeing the words "Hey, sunshine!" But I managed to calm myself down and read on. And what I found was a very short email containing the log-in information for Caleb's YouTube account. In the email, he explained how he had some private videos he wanted me to see, and how he would leave it up to me how I wanted to use those videos.

Immediately, I thought to myself, "Caleb is giving me what I want. He's giving me a chance to hear his voice one more time." And I didn't know if I was ready for that. So I saved the username and password and tucked them away for another day. A stronger day.

Two weeks ago, on New Year's Day, I made a resolution to be stronger. To do more with the awesome gift Caleb bestowed upon me. And the first thing I did was log into that YouTube account.

There are six videos in all. Each one is of him sitting on the stool in his bedroom with his guitar in his lap. He introduces himself and talks about the song he's about to play. The first video I click on is titled "Chasing Abby." And the first time I hear his voice, it's like a kick in the chest.

"I wrote this song after you ran away from me in the mall and you hid in that shoe store. Don't worry. It has nothing to do with malls or shoes. And I'm not actually going to sing the song. The lyrics are in the description, down there." He points downward and I resist the urge to reach out and touch his hand on the screen. "I'm kind of hoping you'll sing while I play, 'cause you know my voice is shit. But you sing like an angel. So, yeah, here it goes. 'Chasing Abby.'"

Today, I'm going to learn how to record a vocal track in Chris's home studio. Today, I'm going to use the many gifts Caleb and the world have offered me. Today, I'm going to sing while Caleb plays.

PART FOUR:

Epilogue

"Chase your dreams, Abby."

EPILOGUE #1

Claire

Seventeen months later

SITTING IN A TRAILER while Abby has her hair and makeup done is surreal. I've only been to three shows where Abby performed, but she wasn't the headliner. So she didn't get her own trailer, which is fine. She's been using Chris's tour bus to play shows all over the country for the past seven months. Chris has been to nineteen of the forty-two shows she's played, which is a lot when you have a new baby in the family.

But Chris has his juggling act down to a science. He's home with me and the kids all week, then he flies out to attend the bigger shows on the weekend. While he's gone, Junior and Ryder help me with Baby Caleb.

Jimi spent the holidays at home in December,

which helped fill the void when Abby spent the holidays with Brian and Lynette at her other grandparents' lodge. The weird thing is that I went eighteen years without Abby, and now I feel empty when I don't get to see her during the holidays. I do wish I would have had more time with her before she went off on tour, but I'm just happy to see her blossom into such a gifted, hardworking performer. And I'm extremely proud that it was Chris who made it all possible. In the end, she needed him as much as he needed her.

Caleb is getting antsy in this trailer. I've taken him for three walks outside since we got here at five p.m., and it's only 6:45. He hates being in confined spaces. He's been sitting on the twin-size bed in the trailer, playing with a box of Legos I brought from home. But now he's grunting and throwing the pieces all over the floor in frustration. Someone's going to step on one of these and sue me.

I scoop him up in my arms and hold him while I kneel down to pick up all the stray Lego pieces. I thought these days were over after Ryder reached a certain age. But it turns out having a new baby in the house has been a blessing in disguise. A very stinky, messy, sickeningly adorable disguise. Even before he was born, Caleb has done a good job of keeping Abby tethered to us. He's very hard to resist.

Abby's personal assistant, Ariana, smiles as she approaches me in the back of the trailer. "Do you need any help, Mrs. Knight? Perhaps a video or something for Caleb to watch?"

"No, thank you, Ariana. Chris will be back soon, then we'll be heading out."

Caleb grabs a red Lego piece out of my hand and stuffs it inside my shirt collar. I laugh as I turn away from Ariana so I can reach inside and dig it out.

"No, Caleb. Stop," I whisper as he tries to put another Lego in my shirt.

"Please let me know if you need anything at all," Ariana says, but when I turn around a few seconds later, she's gone.

I walk about ten steps to the middle of the trailer where Abby is getting her hair done. A woman in a black T-shirt, blue jeans, and a small black apron is styling her hair in perfect beach waves. In her blue peep-toe booties and that silky cream dress, Abby looks more like she stepped off a runway than a beach. But I know I'm just being overprotective. Abby is not a little girl. She's twenty years old. And she's endured way more than most girls her age. She deserves to be doted on and glammed up.

The hairstylist spritzes Abby's hair with a few final squirts of hairspray, then she holds up her arms. "Done!"

"Yay!" Abby cheers, smiling at my reflection in the mirror as she stands from the chair. She turns around and holds her arms out for me to hand Caleb over. "Come here, Bubba."

"He'll ruin your dress, and your hair. That's not a good idea."

"Mm-hmm," the hairstylist agrees with me as she coils the cord around a curling iron.

"Oh, who cares?" Abby protests. "I'm not the star of today's show."

"I beg to differ," I say, handing Caleb to her. "I believe it's *your* name plastered on all the concert posters."

She smiles as she rubs noses with Caleb and he laughs. "You'll agree with me after you see the show."

She plays with Caleb for a few more minutes, then she heads into the bathroom to warm up her vocal folds. She insists on doing this in the bathroom. She thinks it's rude to do it in a roomful of people.

She comes out of the bathroom a few minutes later, as I'm walking Caleb up and down the narrow space running along the center of the trailer. She sits back down in the makeup chair and she suddenly begins to tear up.

"Honey, what's wrong?"

"Nothing," she insists, grabbing a tissue off the makeup counter and dabbing at the corners of her eyes. "I just had a bad vision that I messed up the performance and I let Caleb down."

"Oh, Abby. You could never let him down. Wherever he is, he is so proud of you." I pull Caleb up into my arms and settle him down on my hip. "You've done more with his heart than I'm sure he ever imagined you would do. And I'm sure whatever you have planned for today is going to go perfectly. And if you mess up, I'm sure Caleb will be looking down on you, pointing and laughing."

She lets out a puff of laughter as she wipes her eyes. "You're right. He'd be happy just to see me sitting here talking to you. Thank you."

"You don't have to thank me."

"Yes, I do. I have to thank you. Without you, my parents wouldn't be standing in the front row tonight. Without Chris, I wouldn't even be on that stage. I love you, Mom."

"I never get tired of hearing you call me that. I love

you, sweetheart."

I lean in to kiss her forehead, then I remember I'm wearing lipstick. But when I pull back, Caleb has a chunk of Abby's hair in his hand.

"Oh, no."

I unfurl his fat fingers from around her hair and she smiles as I step back. Then she reaches down and grabs Caleb's hand to walk him up and down the narrow corridor, as I was doing a few minutes ago.

I wish I could tell Abby how much Chris longs to hear her call him Dad. But I know she'll do it when she's ready. She and Chris have spent most of their time together working. I imagine it must be difficult for her to separate all the roles he plays in her life.

As if he can hear my thoughts, Chris enters just as the makeup artist arrives to touch up Abby's makeup. But Abby ignores her. And she's too engrossed in Caleb to see Chris. But Chris's eyes are locked on her, and only one thought crosses my mind.

I don't think there's anyone in this world who loves Abby as fiercely as he does. And you don't need to hold the title Dad to be someone's father. Just as you don't need to be someone's father to hold the title Dad. But when your Dad and your father are both Chris Knight, you can be sure that you're the luckiest girl on the planet.

CHRIS

IT WAS DIFFICULT for Claire to accept that I need to be on the road with Abby this summer. Especially since her forty-first birthday is coming in August, which is also the twenty-fifth anniversary of our first kiss. But she claims she's okay with it now. As long as I'm back before the New Year, our twentieth wedding anniversary.

Where did the time go?

There were so many years, so many endless nights, where it seemed the time would never pass by fast enough to make it to Abby's eighteenth birthday. Now, two years after she walked through my front door, I just want time to slow down. I'm afraid I'll wake up tomorrow and thirty years will have passed, and I'll be scratching my head, wishing I had done more.

But I know this fast-paced life, the long hours in the studio and the touring, will all pay off for Abby.

And in a couple of years, I'll be able to sit back in my recliner and watch her singing the national anthem at the Super Bowl. And I'll smile and say, "That's my princess."

The sound check went great, now I just have to get a good-luck kiss from Claire and this show is sure to go off without a hitch. I race down the steps backstage and make a beeline for Abby's trailer. When I enter, I'm not surprised to find Claire watching as Abby walks little Caleb up and down the tight corridor in the middle of the trailer.

I must admit that I felt vindicated when our fifth child turned out to be a boy. We now outnumber the girls in the house. We have strength in numbers. And it seemed natural that we should let Abby name him, since he was the spark of hope on the horizon for quite a while after Caleb's death.

"Oh, I can't take it. I can't resist those chubby legs!" She scoops him up in her arms and he giggles as she turns him upside-down and gently bites his leg. "Yum!"

There is no sound as beautiful as a child's laughter, but I know the song Abby is going to sing today is going to come pretty damn close. She hands Caleb over to Claire and he laughs as she plants a loud kiss on his cheek.

Claire steps out of the way so Abby can sit down in the makeup chair and the makeup girl scoots around her to do one last touch-up on Abby's face. Abby closes her eyes as a fine dusting of powder is applied to her forehead and cheeks, and I wonder what she's thinking. I hope she's not too nervous.

She's been playing smaller venues for the past seven months in preparation of this album launch. The album released last Tuesday and she's been freaking out for the past four days as she watched the first single, "Chasing Abby," hit the Billboard top ten in its first week. But she's never performed the song live. She wanted to wait until today's show in Raleigh before she unveils something she's been working on for four months with her new boyfriend.

It was odd to me when Abby told me she was dating someone new. I've been wanting her to move on after Caleb's death, but I didn't realize how much Caleb had gotten under my skin until Abby told me about her new beau.

Five months ago, I hired Jaxon Stone to work as a lighting technician on the Chasing Abby Tour. About a month after I hired him, I began noticing Jaxon and Abby sneaking off to have private discussions. At first

I didn't think anything of it. I thought they were just discussing ideas for the lighting. Then, I noticed how sullen Abby looked when Jaxon wasn't around and Jaxon was the same whenever Abby was gone. Finally, I asked Abby what was going on between them and her answer surprised me even more.

"Jaxon is helping me plan a tribute to Caleb."

The smile on her face told me there was more to it than that, but I don't think Abby had admitted this to herself by then. Another month passed and Jaxon was sent away for a couple of weeks to work on a show in Savannah. I saw Abby twice during those two weeks and I've never seen her look so distracted. She was missing marks on the stage, which caused feedback in her earpiece. And the feedback would send her far off pitch. Once Jaxon returned, everything went back to normal. That's when I decided to pull them both aside and find out what was going on.

Like two kids in the principal's office, they both hung their heads when I took them backstage to talk. It took a little coaxing, but eventually they admitted that they were seeing each other outside work. I was skeptical at first. I didn't think it would last more than a month or two. Until I saw what Jaxon and Abby have been planning for tonight's show. I knew then they must be in love. For Jaxon to help her plan this tribute to Caleb and for Abby to allow him to help her tells me they've put a great deal of trust in each other.

The makeup girl finishes powdering Abby's face, and she slides off the chair and turns to me. "I'm so nervous."

I step forward and hold my hand out to her. She reaches out and I pull her into a hug. Her arms wrap around my waist and I kiss her forehead.

"You have nothing to be nervous about. Even if you mess up, I'm sure people will be too busy wiping away their tears to notice." I stroke her hair as I hold her close, reveling in the sensation of her heart beating against my chest. "You ready, princess?"

She shakes her head, so I hold her a while longer until she's so calm I can no longer feel her heart pounding. When she lets me go, I'm surprised to see her smiling.

She lays a soft kiss on my cheek and shrugs. "I guess it's showtime."

I kiss Claire and Caleb, then Abby and I set off through the crowd of crew members scurrying about the grassy field behind the stage. As we approach the steps leading up to the stage, the hum of the crowd gets louder. We stop at the bottom of the stairs and

Abby looks around for Jaxon. Within minutes, he comes bounding out of a pack of lighting techs and Abby sighs with relief as she turns to me.

"Good luck, baby."

"Thanks, Dad."

She kisses my cheek and she and Jaxon set off up the stairs, leaving me in a daze. I'm tempted to reach up and pinch myself to make sure I'm not dreaming, so instead I dig my fists into my pockets. My left hand slides over something smooth and I feel around a bit, trying to figure out what it is. I slide it out of my pocket and find it's a picture.

In the photo, Abby is smiling as she stands in a tattoo parlor. The left strap of her tank top is hanging off her shoulder as she shows off a new tattoo on the left side of her chest. Right over her heart. The tattoo depicts a craggily elm tree with nine blackbirds flying out of the tree and into the sky. One blackbird is left perched in the branches. The trunk of the tree curves downward and the roots bend to form a heart, split down the center by the trunk of the tree. Inside the left side of the heart is the word *Family*. Inside the right side is the word *Music*.

I turn the picture over and there's a note in Abby's handwriting.

Thanks for teaching me about the two most important things in life.

I love you, Dad.

EPILOGUE #2

JAXON AND I race behind the red curtain. A sound tech helps me put on my earpiece. Then a team of crew members helps me up a rolling staircase onto a circular platform as the opening music for the song "Fearless Heart" plays. The screaming in the crowd almost drowns out the music. I blow Jaxon a kiss from atop the platform and he flashes me a proud smile as he backs away.

His dirty-blonde hair and athletic six-foot-two frame disappear behind the backdrop with the other crew members and I know he's in his place when the red lights behind me illuminate the curtain in front of me. A white spotlight behind me casts a silhouette of my body on the curtain as the red lights flash to the beat of the heartbeat in the song. With every beat, a row of fire blasts upward at the front of the stage. The cheering from the crowd is so loud I can feel their screams rattling my insides.

I feel sick to my stomach. My body is breaking out in a cold sweat and my mouth is gushing saliva. Then the sound of the heartbeat stops and the smell of smoke is thick in the air as the curtains part. It's showtime.

Nine songs and three wardrobe changes later, the smell of sweat from the crowd is stronger than the sweet smell of the fog machine. A white screen slowly rolls down behind me as a crew member rushes onto the stage with a wooden stool for me to sit on and a wireless mic for me to hold. He sets down the stool and I hand him my guitar to take backstage. The lights dim and a soft spotlight shines down on me. I take a seat on the stool and sigh into the microphone.

"This next song is going to be the final song of the night." A roar of disapproval erupts from the crowd and I laugh. "I know. But I promise it will be good. You've probably all heard this song before, but I've never performed it live. So you all are seeing the world-premiere performance." I pause for a moment until the cheers die down. "But before I perform this song, I have a story that needs to be told. You see, two years ago today, a very special person helped me find the other half of my broken heart. And a few months later, when my heart was completely shattered beyond repair, he gave me his. The world never got to know Caleb Everett's talent, as he was taken from us far too soon. But after tonight, everyone will know him. And to know him is to love him. Take it away, Caleb."

Four different projectors blast rays of light through the smoky air, all focused on a spot to my right. Within seconds, a hazy image begins to form and soon a hologram of Caleb appears next to me. He's sitting on a stool in his bedroom with his guitar in his lap. The hologram is so well defined, he looks real. Like I could just reach out and touch him and he'd respond.

Jaxon and I had to write a proposal to the director of the physics department at USC to request to use their ultra-high-definition holographic projectors. Jimi presented the proposal for us. She's an actress and she has more poise in her pinky than Jaxon and I have in our whole bodies. Together, we managed to get USC to let us use their projectors.

Jaxon and I have been fine-tuning the audio and video feed for the past four months. He's also been working with the rest of the lighting crew to program the projectors and the light show for this performance. Possibly, the most important performance of my life. It only makes sense that Caleb should be there to see me through it.

The crowd gets very quiet and Caleb looks up from his guitar. "I'm kind of hoping you'll sing while I play, 'cause you know my voice is shit. But you sing like an angel. So, yeah, here it goes. 'Chasing Abby.'"

He plucks out a soft melancholy melody on his guitar and my hands start shaking as I sing the first line.

You're the sun that shines down on this carnival of hearts.
The ray of light that breaks through when the curtains part.
You're the healing breath waiting for me to surface.
The spark of hope that lights me up with just a kiss.
But you're just beyond the horizon.
Yeah, just beyond my reach.
An ocean between us and I can't,
Can't find a ship on this beach.

And I'll keep standing on this shore,
Hoping the light will catch me.
Send up smoke signals you can't ignore,
But I'll keep chasing Abby.
'Cause time catches up with everyone,
So I'll catch up with Abby

All through the streets and down the broken lanes.
All across the years, time and time again.
Your heart keeps me yearning, through the ages.
Your love keeps me learning, flipping pages.
But you're just beyond the scope,
And this ship hasn't breached.
You keep dangling the hope,
Just out of my reach.

And I'll keep standing on this shore,
Hoping the light will catch me.
Send up smoke signals you can't ignore,
But I'll keep chasing Abby.
'Cause time catches up with everyone,
So I'll catch up with Abby.

When I sailed the seas and found you huddled just beyond the signs,
Thought I'd found the grail, but turns out all I found was my sunshine.
I knew then that your heart would never really belong to me,
Because blackbirds can't touch the sky if you never set them free.

And I'll keep standing on this shore,
Hoping the light will catch me.
Send up smoke signals you can't ignore,
But I'll keep chasing Abby.
'Cause time catches up with everyone,
So I'll catch up with Abby.
Fly away, my little sunshine.
Fly away where I can't see.

Caleb stands from his stool and I stand up with him. He takes a bow and his hologram disappears into the foggy mist. I take a bow, wishing I could stay in this position so people can't see the tears streaming down my face. I stand up and hold my fist over my heart. Then I close my eyes and thank Caleb for giving me wings.

After a twenty-minute encore where I perform three more tracks, including another of Caleb's songs that's not on the album, I bid the audience goodnight and head to the grassy field behind the stage. As expected, Chris, Claire, and Caleb; both my parents; and Jaxon are waiting for me at the foot of the stairs. Since we started sharing holidays together, both sets of parents have become quite friendly. They've even had dinner together without my knowledge a couple of times since I went on tour.

Amy isn't here, but she's promised me she'll be attending tomorrow night's show. I am a bit surprised to see Jimi, Junior, and Ryder standing right beside Chris and Claire. Jimi wasn't supposed to be back from California until next week and Junior and Ryder insisted they were staying home tonight to pack their stuff to go to the beach house tomorrow.

My mom approaches me first for a hug. "That was amazing, honey," she says, squeezing me tightly. "You looked so beautiful up there. And that last song... it took my breath away. I'm so proud of you."

"Thanks, Mom."

Everyone else takes turns hugging and congratulating me until the only ones left are Jimi and Jaxon. Jimi approaches me with tears in her eyes and just the sight of it makes me feel like crying, but I keep my composure.

"Well, I don't know what to say after all that, other than… thanks for letting me be a small part of this. I've been to a lot of shows with Dad, but I think this one tops them all. You were fucking phenomenal, sis. Caleb would probably do a pirouette if he saw that."

I laugh and she hugs me a bit longer than everyone else. I can't believe how much has changed in two years. Today, Jimi is the one person I will miss the most while Chris and I are on the road this summer. But there's one person I won't have to miss. And when I let Jimi go, Jaxon is standing there, wearing a crooked smile that fills me with both joy and sorrow.

Jaxon knew from the day we met that he had some big shoes to fill. Which is why, though we met almost a year and a half after Caleb's death, it still took two months of flirting for him to work up the nerve to ask me out. And even then, it took three dates for him to try to kiss me.

I don't blame him, though. When we first met, my favorite topic was Caleb. And there's never a family gathering where he's not mentioned. But Jaxon has one of the kindest, gentlest souls I've ever had the pleasure of knowing. And he's always encouraging me to remember Caleb. Not just for the gifts he gave me, but for teaching me how to give and receive love.

Jaxon holds his hand out to me and I'm reminded of Caleb's lyrics: *"I knew then that your heart would never really belong to me / Because blackbirds can't touch the sky if you never set them free."* My heart will always belong to Caleb. But Jimi is right. Wherever Caleb is, he's beaming with pride because I got up on that stage tonight and gave my heart—*his heart*—to the music. And I danced like he was the only one watching.

Turn the page for a preview of

RIPPED

A Shattered Hearts Series Novel

nothing could tear
them apart...

until now.

A Shattered Hearts Series Novel

RIPPED

NEW YORK TIMES BESTSELLING AUTHOR
CASSIA LEO

CHAPTER ONE

Adam

(Disclaimer: This excerpt is unedited and subject to change or deletion from the final book.)

I approach slowly, not wanting to anger it, then I position my shoe in just the right spot before I bring it down fast on top of the cockroach. A sickening crunch tells me I destroyed him, but Lindsay still cowers on the bed, her back against the headboard and knees hugged tightly to her chest. I slowly remove my size-thirteen sneaker from the wall where the three-inch-long flying cockroach was perched.

It twitches slightly and Lindsay lets out a shrill scream. "I hate this resort!"

The 80-percent-dead roach falls to the floor on its back and makes a half-hearted effort to turn itself over.

Lindsay continues to scream. "Don't just stare at it. Put it out of its misery! It's suffering!"

I shake my head. "Sorry, little guy. But you have to die or I'll never have sex tonight. It's survival of the fittest."

I swat the roach one last time, then I scoop it up with some toilet paper and flush it away. After I wash off the bottom of my shoe, I come out of the bathroom ready to consummate our unofficial second honeymoon. But Lindsay is curled up on her side, hugging herself.

"Come on, baby. It was just one monster-sized flying roach." I sit on the edge of the bed and push her blonde hair out of her face. "We're on the edge of a rainforest. There's probably critters in all the hotel rooms in this area. I'll bet they even serve the roaches as a delicacy at the Four Seasons."

"You're literally making me sick with fear."

The bungalow on the beach in Bahia is one of the shittiest rooms we've stayed in since I began surfing competitively seven years ago. Seven years. I can't believe I was afraid my dad would tell me twenty-three was too old to start competing again after a two-year hiatus. Well, I'm thirty now and at the top of my game. So why the fuck am I staying in a shitty room like this?

It's all my fault.

The resort sold me a package, which included a bungalow on the sand and a couples' massage in their "five-diamond" spa. I'm not allowed to get a massage from anyone other than Edie, my sports physician. But

I thought Lindsay would appreciate it. And I was afraid if I didn't book the package right away, Lindsay would change her mind about coming with me.

She's only three-months pregnant with our third, but she's already mega-stressed about this child. Our youngest, Mila, is still in diapers. But now that our oldest, Kaia, is in second grade, we decided to put her in a private school in Wilmington. We weren't happy with the two tutors we'd hired to homeschool her, and Lindsay doesn't feel confident her English degree is sufficient to teach the kids herself. This means we had to sell the beach house and move to Wilmington. It also means that, from now on, I'll be traveling to competitions all over the world alone.

This tournament in Bahia, Brazil is officially the last one Lindsay will be attending with me. Which is why we decided to come here alone. We left the kids with Lindsay's mom, Lillian, for five days while we enjoy our moldy bungalow "just steps from the beach." I have to be at the beach at seven in the morning tomorrow for the tournament, and I always perform better when I've had sex the night before.

I'm going to have to seduce her.

I tuck a lock of Lindsay's hair behind her ear and she shudders. She always gets goosebumps when I touch her ears. I trace my fingers lightly down her jawline until I reach her chin.

I gently grab her chin between my thumb and forefinger and turn her head so she's facing me. "I'm sorry this resort sucks." I lean down and plant a soft kiss on her lips, then I pull away just far enough so our noses are still touching and she can feel my breath on her lips. "But I think I know how I can make it up to you."

She lets out a soft puff of laughter. "This isn't going to work, Adam. The moment passed. I just want to go to sleep. Actually, I just want this trip to be over. If you really want to make it up to me, you can fast-forward through the next three days."

This is the longest Lindsay has ever been away from the girls. We were supposed to take an eight-day honeymoon after we got married, but Lindsay's constant worrying about Kaia caused us to cut the trip to three days. Lindsay frets over the kids feeling our absence; especially mine. Since Kaia's biological father died when she was just a couple of months old, Lindsay believes it's important for the girls not to feel as if I'm a temporary presence in their lives.

I've been away from the kids for as long as eleven days at a time. Sometimes, tournaments are scheduled so close together, it makes more sense to travel straight from one location to the next instead of making a pit stop at home in between. Those are the competitions Lindsay refuses to attend. It's hard enough to travel with two children. But when you add Mila, it's just too much.

That's a joke Lindsay would appreciate, me referring to myself as a child. You have to have a childlike sense of adventure when you get paid to surf. When people who don't recognize me ask what I do for a living, I always tell them I get paid to play in the ocean. Of course, it's getting more difficult to find people who don't recognize me.

I stand from the mattress and round the bed to go to the other side. "Okay, let's go to sleep."

I slide in under the covers, but I don't bother to turn off the bedside lamp. I scoot in closer to Lindsay so I can spoon her, then I brush her hair away from her neck and curl my arm around her waist.

Sliding my hand just under the waistband of her panties, I hold my hand over her abdomen. "I can't wait to meet this little guy."

"You don't even know if it's a boy," she replies, laying her hand over my hand and threading her fingers through mine.

I nuzzle my face into the curve of her neck. "Don't argue with me, or I'll force you to go without sex tonight."

I lay a tender kiss on the soft skin behind her ear and her fingers tighten around my hand. "I really wanted this to be a romantic getaway for us."

I run the tip of my nose along the outer curve of her ear and she sighs. "We can pretend that we're stranded on a deserted island and I built this shitty bungalow myself with my bulging muscles." She chuckles and I squeeze her tighter. I love the sound of her laughter. "Hey, remember when you were watching me build this bungalow? You were lying on the beach... naked. Because we lost all our clothes when our plane went down in the ocean. You should take off these panties. They're making it difficult to recall this memory."

I slide my hand farther down and she sucks in a sharp breath when my finger glides over her clit. I slip my finger inside her and I'm not surprised to find she's soaking wet. She's always horny when she's pregnant. All it takes is a dirty word or a come-hither expression to get her slick.

I feel around inside her a little, searching for her g-spot and I know I've found it when her whole body twitches. She lifts her hips a little so she can push down her panties, but I keep my finger locked inside her. Once her panties are gone, she reaches down and pulls my hand out from between her legs.

"What are you doing?"

She turns around to face me, then she begins pushing my boxers down. "I can't let you lose tomorrow or this awful trip won't be worth it. Lie back."

She shoves my shoulder and I turn onto my back as I kick my boxers off. She straddles one of my thighs and the wetness of her pussy on my skin makes me even harder. I smile as she rubs herself on me a little before she leans forward and takes my dick into her mouth.

Her mouth is warm and her lips form a firm O-ring around my cock as she bobs up and down for a few minutes. She pulls me out of her mouth and smiles as she gently slides her tongue up and down along the slit at the tip. Then she uses the tip of her tongue to stimulate the sensitive ridge under the head.

She sits up and smiles as she mounts me slowly, so I can feel every ridge inside her. "I think I remember now," she says, leaning forward so she can kiss my neck. "Your hard, naked body was dripping sweat as you were building the walls of the bungalow."

"And you were lying on the beach, touching yourself as you watched me *hammering* the studs… and flexing my rippling muscles."

"Mm-hmm," she murmurs with a slight chuckle as she slides her hand between us to reach her clit.

I grab her hips and thrust into her as she moves up and down on my cock. "And then I decided to take a break from building so I could help out with the housework."

She laughs and sits up straight so she can touch herself while I thrust my hips beneath her. "What kind of housework?"

I smile as I grab her breasts, rolling her nipples and massaging her flesh. "I cooked you a romantic dinner of plantains and coconut *and* I cleaned the machete."

"Oh, God," she moans, throwing her head back as she continues to caress her clit.

I chuckle as I reach up, take her face in my hands, and roughly pull her forward so I can kiss her deeply. I bite her top lip and she whimpers. I flip her onto her back and suck on her neck as I move slowly in and out of her.

I bring my lips right next to her and whisper, "Then I made a bed of grass for you to lie down while

I impregnated you with my super sperm." She laughs, but she quickly stops when I trace the tip of my tongue along the inner shell of her ear. "Don't laugh. It's a delicate procedure. Do you want me to show you how it's done?"

"Absolutely."

I slip my cock out of her and slide down so I can take her firm nipple into my mouth. She moans as I suck on her flesh, her hips bucking against my chest. I slide farther down and trace a circle around her navel with my tongue, then I lay a soft kiss on her abdomen.

"The first step involves multiple orgasms. Are you ready?"

"Yes," she whispers breathlessly.

She got a Brazilian wax for our trip and I smile as I spread her flesh and lick a straight line from her entrance to her clit. She whimpers as I suck gently on her glistening jewel. She gasps as I slide two fingers inside her pussy and massage her g-spot while swirling my tongue around her clit.

I look up at her to see her reaction, but her back is arched so deeply, all I can see are the soft peaks of her breasts. I stop moving my fingers for a moment, focusing just on her hard nub until her body begins to tremble. Then I pull my mouth away and just massage her g-spot. When she begins to squirm, I remove my fingers from inside her and lightly flick her clit with the tip of my tongue. The orgasm is so intense, I'm pretty sure she woke all the animals in the rainforest with her screaming.

I move up to slide my cock back inside her, when I see something on her side. I lean my head to the left to get a better look and realize it's a fucking tick.

"Don't move," I warn her.

Her chest is heaving as she tries to catch her breath. "Why?"

"You have a tick on your side."

"*WHAT?*"

She kicks me as she flails about and jumps out of the bed. She twists her neck this way and that, trying to get a look at it, but she can't view it from this angle.

"Calm down and don't try to take it out yourself. I'll get it out."

"Are you fucking kidding me? This better be a joke!" she shrieks as she races to the bathroom to look in the mirror. "Oh, my God! I have a tick! Get it out! Hurry!"

"Calm down, baby. I have to call the concierge to see if they can get us a lighter."

"A lighter! You're going to burn me? What is this,

the fucking dark ages? Do not even *think* about burning me. I want to go to the hospital."

I pick up the phone on the desk and dial the concierge. "Yes, my wife just discovered a tick on her body," I begin as I attempt to make my erection go away. "Are you aware that there are ticks and cockroaches in these bungalows?"

"Good evening, sir. Would you like us to send you a tick removal kit?"

Less than an hour later, Edie arrives with her medical bag and the tick removal kit she picked up at the front desk for us. She removes the tick for Lindsay and cleans the wound, then she hands her a box of azithromycin (antibiotics.) She drops the tick into a zipped plastic bag so she can have it tested when we get back to the States. When Edie's gone, Lindsay heads straight to the closet and pulls out our empty blue suitcase.

"What are you doing?"

"I'm leaving."

She heaves the suitcase onto the bed and I grab the handle to pull it away from her. "Come on. Let's just go to sleep and we'll change hotel rooms after the tournament tomorrow."

"Easy for you to say. You're not the one who's

possibly been infected with Lyme disease!"

I curl my arm around her waist and take her breast in my hand as I pull her away from the bed. "I don't know why you're complaining. Lyme disease goes so well with coconut fever." I squeeze her breast and she stomps on my foot. "Fuck!"

"I'll give you coconut fever." I immediately cover my nuts as she rounds on me, but she just shakes her head and goes straight to the bathroom. "I'm going to take a shower. And I'm not going to your tournament tomorrow. I'm going to spend the day changing our itinerary. We're leaving Brazil tomorrow night. And we're not taking any of our clothes back with us."

I follow her into the bathroom and watch as she angrily rips off her clothing and turns on the shower. "I can't leave tomorrow night and you know that. The sponsor dinner is the following night. Anyone who places has to be there."

"Then you can stay and I'll leave. And your daughters can wonder where you are while you're getting drunk with the sponsors."

She steps inside the shower, so I raise my voice to be heard over the water. "That's not fair. I don't want to leave them anymore then they want me gone."

"Then don't leave them. Quit. It's not as if we

need the money."

This is not the first time Lindsay and I have discussed me quitting. We talked a lot about it this year while we were trying to get pregnant and while enrolling Kaia in her new school. But I always got the feeling that she wanted me to do what would make me happiest. Right now, I'm getting a strong feeling she wants me to put my happiness aside for the kids' sake.

It's not an unreasonable demand to make. But the thought of quitting the competitions fills me with a deep hopelessness; something I haven't felt since before we got back together seven years ago.

I peel off my clothes and step into the shower with her. I take the tiny shampoo bottle out of her hand and place it back on the shelf. Then I take her face in my hands and kiss her tenderly. Within seconds, she begins to cry.

"I just want you to be there for them."

"I know." I kiss her forehead and let out a deep sigh. "I'll do it. I'll quit."

To purchase RIPPED, please visit:
cassialeo.com/ripped

Chasing Abby Playlist

Prologue
"The Broken Ones" by Dia Frampton

Chapter One
"Cool Kids (Acoustic)" by Echosmith

Chapter Four
"Blackbird" by Sarah McLachlan

Chapter Five
"Two Is Better Than One" by Boys Like Girls, Taylor Swift

Chapter Seven
"Let's Love (Acoustic)" by Echosmith
"You're My Best Friend" by Queen
"Blackbird" by The Beatles

Chapter Nine
"Somewhere Only We Know" by Lily Allen

Chapter Ten
"Talking Dreams (Acoustic)" by Echosmith

Chapter Twelve
"Pray" Kodaline

Chapter Thirteen
"The Reason (Acoustic)" by Hoobastank

Chapter Fourteen
"Terminal (Acoustic)" by Echosmith

Chapter Seventeen
"Adore You" by Miley Cyrus

Chapter Eighteen
"No Ordinary Love (Live)" by The Civil Wars

Chapter Nineteen
"A Sky Full of Stars" by Coldplay

Chapter Twenty
"Imagine" by John Lennon
"Little Wing" by Jimi Hendrix

Chapter Twenty-Two
"Collide - Acoustic Version" by Howie Day

Chapter Twenty-Three

"Tell Her You Love Her Too (Acoustic)" by
Echosmith

Chapter Twenty-Five
"Hallelujah - Live at KCRW.com" by Brandi Carlile

Chapter Twenty-Six
"Apologize - Acoustic Version" Kacey Musgraves

Chapter Twenty-Seven
"Crazy in Love" Daniela Andrade

Chapter Twenty-Eight
"Godspeed (Sweet Dreams)" by Dixie Chicks

Chapter Twenty-Nine
"Fast Car" by Kina Grannis

Chapter Thirty
"Bullet Train – Acoustic Version" by Stephen Swartz,
Joni Fatora

Chapter Thirty-Two
"Fuel to Fire" by Agnes Obel

Chapter Thirty-Three
"Wild Horses" by The Rolling Stones

Epilogue #1
"How Long Will I Love You" by Ellie Goulding

Epilogue #2
"In My Life" by The Beatles

Listen to the playlist on YouTube.
bit.ly/chasingabbyplaylist

Listen to the playlist on Spotify.
bit.ly/chasingabbyplaylists

Chasing Abby

You're the sun that shines down on this carnival of hearts.
The ray of light that breaks through when the curtains part.
You're the healing breath waiting for me to surface.
The spark of hope that lights me up with just a kiss.
But you're just beyond the horizon.
Yeah, just beyond my reach.
An ocean between us and I can't,
Can't find a ship on this beach.

And I'll keep standing on this shore,
Hoping the light will catch me.
Send up smoke signals you can't ignore,
But I'll keep chasing Abby.
'Cause time catches up with everyone,
So I'll catch up with Abby

All through the streets and down the broken lanes.
All across the years, time and time again.
Your heart keeps me yearning, through the ages.
Your love keeps me learning, flipping pages.
But you're just beyond the scope,
And this ship hasn't breached.
You keep dangling the hope,

Just out of my reach.

And I'll keep standing on this shore,
Hoping the light will catch me.
Send up smoke signals you can't ignore,
But I'll keep chasing Abby.
'Cause time catches up with everyone,
So I'll catch up with Abby.

When I sailed the seas and found you huddled
just beyond the signs,
Thought I'd found the grail, but turns out all I found
was my sunshine.
I knew then that your heart would never really belong to me,
Because blackbirds can't touch the sky if you never set them free.

And I'll keep standing on this shore,
Hoping the light will catch me.
Send up smoke signals you can't ignore,
But I'll keep chasing Abby.
'Cause time catches up with everyone,
So I'll catch up with Abby.
Fly away, my little sunshine.
Fly away where I can't see.

Acknowledgements

FIRST AND FOREMOST, I have to thank my beta readers: Jordana Rodriguez, Paula Jackman, Kristin Shaw, Carrie Raasch, Sarah Arndt, and Cathy Archer. Thank you so much for taking this journey with me.

Thanks again to Sarah Hansen at Okay Creations. Thanks for helping me fix this cover. I'm very grateful for your patience and expertise.

Thank you to Marianne Tatom for fitting me in and doing such an amazing job finding my million typos.

Huge thank-you to all the book bloggers who have shared the Shattered Hearts series with your friends, families, and readers. Thank you for sharing the teasers and cover reveal. Thank you for supporting me and my books. Thank you for making my life easier. Especially you, Holly Malgieri!

My daughter for encouraging me to continue writing whenever I'm ready to give up (every day.)

And, last but not least, a huge thank-you to my street

team, Cassia's Kittens, and all the readers who have shared my books, cheered me on, and begged for more. Even the ones who challenged me and drove me up the wall so I'd write this book. Thanks for bugging the crap out of me.

Other books by Cassia Leo

CONTEMPORARY ROMANCE

Relentless (Shattered Hearts #1)

Pieces of You (Shattered Hearts #2)

Bring Me Home (Shattered Hearts #3)

Abandon (Shattered Hearts #3.5)

Black Box (stand-alone novel)

PARANORMAL ROMANCE

Parallel Spirits (Carrier Spirits #1)

EROTIC ROMANCE

Unmasked Series

KNOX Series

LUKE Series

CHASE Series

Get Involved

Sign up for Cassia's mailing list to
stay up to date on all new releases, deals,
bonus content, giveaways, cover reveals, and more!
cassialeo.com/news

Or text BOOKLOVE to 41411

to be notified of new book releases

**Want to discuss the books with Cassia
and other readers?**

Join the Shattered Hearts Discussion Group
http://bit.ly/shatteredhearts

About the Author

New York Times and *USA Today* bestselling author Cassia Leo loves her coffee, chocolate, and margaritas with salt. When she's not writing, she spends way too much time watching old reruns of *Friends* and *Sex and the City*. When she's not watching reruns, she's usually enjoying the California sunshine or reading—sometimes both.

Made in the USA
Middletown, DE
15 October 2014